GENERATION DEAD

BOOK TWO, WHAT YOU FEAR

JOSEPH TALLUTO

ISBN: 978-1-925047-37-0

CHAPTER 1

"Do you see them?"

"No. Am I supposed to?"

"Are you looking?"

"In case it's escaped your notice, it's really dark out here."

"That's a no, then?"

"Well, if they're out here, they'll hear you for sure."

"Fine. Be that way."

My brother Jake was a pain in the ass, but since he was consistently a pain in the ass, it was easier to handle. However, there were times, *this* being one of them, that his signature resemblance to a person's posterior was really annoying.

We were standing on a bike path directly underneath a bridge in St. Charles, and we were hunting zombies. Not exactly, the way I'd like to be spending my evenings, but since we decided to be the saviors of the new country, we had to go where the action was, and that brought us to St. Charles.

Before this, we were collectors, going into forbidden zones and zombie infested territory to bring back a piece of the life other people left behind when they fled the first hordes of undead. However, circumstances forced us to take a hard look at what we were doing and why we were doing it, and we changed course rather suddenly. We realized we were trained for a different purpose, not just to go after other people's crap. Our father had spent years making sure we could survive attacks by any person, alive or dead, and we had come to the realization that we were meant to do something bigger than ourselves.

"Jesus, it's dark tonight. Do you think we're nuts for being out here?" Jake wondered.

I was glad he couldn't see my face. Otherwise, he might have been offended by the severe eye rolling I was giving him at the moment.

"Slightly. It's darker than hell out here. I can't hear a thing, thanks to the river next to me, and we're chasing zombies along a bike path at night. I'm not sure which part of that might qualify for sanity," I said.

"Good point. Well, I...wait. Did you see that?" Jake peered forward and stared hard at the shadows.

I looked in the general direction that he did, although I didn't stare directly at the same spot. At night, you could actually see better using your peripheral vision. That was something Julia's father had taught us years ago. I couldn't see anything at first, but then it became clearer. Something was moving along the path, and it was slow enough to be a concern.

"Got it. Think it's a zombie?" I asked.

"Only one way to find out," Jake said, moving forward. I followed at a slight distance, not wanting to crowd him if he began swinging his melee weapon. It was a three-foot length of wood, topped by a few blunt pyramids of steel. It was brutally effective on zombie skulls, and not nearly as messy as mine.

My weapon for this evening was a falchion. It was a sword with a single edge and a drop point made for stabbing. It was sharp enough to cut a zombie in half, and I had done just that several times since acquiring it. It was a butcher's blade, no finesse about it. It was meant to hack and slash, and it did both with equal enthusiasm. I used it sparingly, preferring to take on zombies with my knife and tomahawk, but given the darkness we were in, I couldn't hope to be as precise as I needed to be with either of those weapons.

Jake moved quietly, hoping to get a kill in before the zombie saw him and raised a groan. He stepped around trees, keeping to the soft grass growing by the path. The sound of the river was constant, and helped masked our approach. The trees provided a darker cover for us, and the cloudy sky helped make things even darker. Zombies couldn't see very well at night, and they processed what they saw fairly slowly. Nevertheless, they hunted at night through sound and smell, and those two senses were enough.

Jake made it to a tree and peered around cautiously. I was about fifteen feet back in the grass, ready to lend a hand, but I knew Jake wouldn't have any trouble with a lone zombie.

Turns out, I was right. The ghoul shuffled along, oblivious to the danger, and never saw the mace that swung out from a tree and crushed its skull. The zombie, a young male, let out a single croak as its unlife left it, then collapsed to the ground.

Jake looked at the zombie for a second, and then stepped out onto the path.

"Not too hard," he whispered.

"Don't get cocky," I whispered back. "There's some movement by that big gazebo over there." I pointed into the gloom with my sword and something was definitely over by the big grandstand gazebo that occupied a small peninsula on the river.

"After you," said Jake.

"Too kind."

We made our way carefully along the path, making sure we didn't step on any twigs or acorns. Since it was so dark, it wasn't easy, so we had to slide our feet along. Since that was going to cause noise, we had to do it carefully. Every step became a much longer exercise than just walking along, taking in the night air.

As we moved, I thought about what brought us here. Our world had been turned upside down by the coming of the Enillo Virus and the resulting rise of the dead. Billions died in the aftermath, and the world was pretty much over for anyone in the breathing category. However, a few hardy souls, our father among them, decided not to go quietly to the grave, and fought back, carving out an existence on the backs of the undead. It took a concentrated effort, and a lot of sacrifice, but the country was saved and essentially starting over. We'd had peace for nearly sixteen years, but someone had decided that it was more fun to see if they could turn the clock back. We found evidence of a deliberate outbreak, and realized we were probably the only ones who were trained enough to handle it. The first outbreak was aimed directly at us, and we found it wasn't thrilling to wake and be surrounded by townsfolk that were living the night before but no longer.

Once that was finished, we discovered another outbreak where one shouldn't have been, and that brought us to this bike path in the middle of the night. We'd arrived too late to save the whole town, but we managed to corral the rest away from the zombies, and by the time that was done, we were looking at darkness. We couldn't hold up for the night, since there were living communities directly to the south and north of us, and as the river was right here, that was the only way the zombies were going to go.

We really didn't have a choice but to go out and hunt the damn things. As we moved, I wondered again whether our dad felt like this when he was in a crazy situation not of his own making.

"On your right," Jake whispered.

I looked carefully and saw a pair of zombies making their way through the long grass. They were difficult to see, but I could tell by their pale skin that they were relatively fresh kills. New zombies tended to be very pale around the face, as the blood drained and pooled in the lower part of the body after death. In the darkness, they nearly glowed.

I slipped into the grass and crouched as I stalked them. The noise of the river was reassuring, and the breeze on my face made sure they couldn't smell me. However, I could smell them, and they were already giving off that sickly-sweet smell of death. It was like nothing else, and once you caught wind of it, you never forgot it.

I waited until they were close, and did so while crouched among the grass and leaves. It was a pain to wait, but it meant I controlled the encounter from start to finish. Give the zombies an inch and they will rip your throat out.

When they were within four feet of me, I suddenly stood up, bringing my sword up in a two-handed strike from the ground. The blade caught the nearest zombie right at the jawline, and cut her head off in a single stroke. With the blade high, I took a step towards the second zombie, a thin man of about twenty. He stepped towards me at the same time, bringing him within reach. My sword split his skull easily, and dropped him with barely a whisper. I poked around with my sword tip until I found the other zombie's still moving head, and finished it with a quick stab to the eye.

I moved back to Jake and waited while he dispatched a big zombie on his side. He didn't finesse the thing at all. He just stood there, waiting for the zombie to come to him, and then he jumped and brought his mace down with a crunch on the big guy's head. The zombie fell like a tree, smacking heavily on the bike path.

"Shh!" I whispered. "You trying to attract attention and get a horde?"

"So sorry," Jake said sarcastically. "Next time, I'll ask him to politely lie down while I bash his brains in."

"Please do." I pointed with my sword at another trio of zombies that were attracted to the noise, and were coming to investigate.

"Great. All right. I'll wait here, and you go by that tree. When they pass, come up behind and cut them down."

"Sounds like a plan." I slipped over to the tree he had indicated and peeked around the trunk. Three zombies, about four feet apart, were making their way quickly towards my brother. In a few seconds, they would be past me. I ducked back around the tree and listened for them to pass. As I did, I readied my sword, holding it up by my shoulder, with my hands in the hilt about chest high.

That posture saved me. I heard the zombies go past, and then I moved around the big tree. I was all set to kill some zombies when I ran smack into one. Apparently, this one had seen me and was coming to see why I wanted to be alone. I bounced into her and she grabbed at me as she fell back. Her hands grabbed my sword blade and they were immediately cut to the bone. I whipped the steel away and managed to slice three of her fingers off. Her other hand grabbed at my shirt, and she tried to pull me in for a bite while her diced hand futilely grabbed at my arm.

I put a hand on her chest and pushed her against the tree, dropping my sword and plucking my tomahawk from its sheath on my belt. I didn't have much room for a swing, being stuck holding a zombie chick against a tree, so I choked up on the handle, reversed the blade so the spike was to the front, and jammed the point into the forehead of the zombie. A quick twist and she was done, sliding down the tree to the ground.

I grabbed up my sword and ran around the tree, finding Jake, who was finishing off his two attackers.

"Sorry, the girl surprised me." I said, by way of apology.

Jake shrugged. "No worries. I saw her angle off, so I figured it wasn't going to go as planned."

I thought about that for a minute. "Wait. Why didn't you warn me?"

Jake pointed to the gazebo. "That's why."

I glanced over and saw several zombies milling about the gazebo. In truth, it really wasn't a gazebo; it was a small outdoor stage. Nevertheless, it was designed to look like one so that's what we called it.

"Think they're here to do *Hamlet*? I asked.

"Why not? Everyone's dead at the end of that play, too. Let's move around these trees and see what we can do about this."

We crept back to the grass and kept low, trying to stay out of sight. It worked for the most part, but then the zombies started to get agitated. They began moving faster and started coming off the stage. Every single one was headed in our direction.

"What the hell?" Jake whispered. "Did you make a noise?"

"Did you hear one? No, stupid, the wind is at our backs. They can smell us," I said. "Get ready."

We split apart and stood about twenty feet from each other. This was going to get messy in a hurry. Jake rolled his shoulders and I popped my neck and arms. We couldn't run, they'd locked onto us and we had nowhere really to go. The brush on the other side of the bike path was thicker than Jake's skull and might as well have been a stone wall.

As the first few zombies began to approach our position, I began to hear strange sounds, as if someone was cracking walnuts. It didn't make any sense so I didn't mention it to Jake. Besides, the game was on and I had zombies to slice.

The first one in line was an easy kill. I just thrust the point through their open mouth and kicked them off my blade as they fell. The second one got its left leg cut off at the knee, spilling it to the ground. I moved away so as not to be distracted by a crawler. To the side, I could hear Jake cracking skulls, and piling up kills on his own. A smaller zombie, probably a kid about fifteen years old, stumbled through the grass at a decent clip, and caused me to time my swing incorrectly. Instead of slamming into his skull, the big blade cut deeply into his collarbone. The blade stuck, and I didn't have time to yank it out. The teenager grabbed at me and the hilt of my sword, while another two came barreling out of the darkness on my right. Crap. I hauled the zombie around and blocked the advance of the nearest oncoming zombie by stabbing it in the chest with the blade still sticking out of my first one. The second zombie lurched at me and I dodged its arms, bumping it with my hip and knocking it to the ground. I shoved hard on the sword, pushing over my two pinned zombies and pinning them to the ground with the sword.

I didn't have time to admire my handiwork, since the third one was up and moving. I grabbed my tomahawk from its sheath and pulled my knife from its place one my belt. As the zombie reached up, I backhanded the tomahawk into its head and I was rewarded with a crack that put it down for good. That solved my closest concern. Another zombie was headed my way when it suddenly stopped moving and fell face first into the grass.

Huh. That was weird. I looked around and saw only one person still standing by the stage. Jake was done with his supply of zombies and he was coming over to finish off the two that were still writhing on the ground. Two cracks later, and we were done. I yanked out my sword and wiped off the blood and gore as well as I could. Walking over to the stage, I approached the figure still standing there. Several shapes were still on the ground, and they obviously had been dispatched with extreme prejudice.

As I reached the stage, the figure suddenly took two steps forward and jumped at me! I brought up an arm and caught the person as they landed on me, swinging my sword wide and out of the way. The person wiggled and wrapped their legs around my waist, and I felt teeth on my ear.

CHAPTER 2

"Gotcha," was all that was whispered.

I turned my head and kissed Julia. "Yes, you do." I put her down and she smiled up at me. Even in the darkness, I could see her smile. "Weren't you supposed to stay with the community until we got back?" I asked.

Julia's smile vanished. "The local response team finally showed up, so I went out to find you guys. I got chased by the group we just killed, and was on the roof of the gazebo, wondering what the hell I was going to do until morning, when you guys distracted them and I was able to get down and lend a hand."

Jake wandered over just as Julia finished her speech. "Take a breath. How come you let yourself get cornered?"

Julia frowned. "Don't be an ass. I would have jumped to the river in the morning if they were still around."

Jake considered that and shrugged. I thought it made sense, but I wasn't going to admit it out loud and cause tension.

Jake surprised me with his next statement. "Anyway, thanks for the assist. We've taken care of twenty-three of these new ones, which leaves fifteen unaccounted for. At least, according to what the locals have told us."

"True, there's been enough time to contaminate others and they're just completing the transformation process right about now, so we might be busy a little while longer," I said.

"Which means we should get moving and check the other side of the river." Julia said.

"Let's use that bridge." Jake said, pointing to an immense structure further south along the river. Even in the darkness, I could see its massive pylons and heavy steel beams. It struck me as very curious as to why such a bridge was made for a little thing like a bike path.

We moved along quickly and quietly. I was actually very happy to see Julia, but then these days I was happy to see her all the time. She and I had grown up together, and until recently, I had really thought of her as a sister. But we had grown closer lately, and I discovered my feelings for her had become a lot deeper than I realized. Imagine my surprise when I discovered she had the same feelings for me.

Jake was in the lead, and we could just make out his dark shape as we moved along. I whispered to Julia as we walked.

"How are things with the survivors?" I asked.

"Pretty good. They're shaken up, wondering where the virus came from. They've been pretty good about keeping themselves safe, suddenly waking up and finding new zombies wondering around that yesterday used to be your neighbor or brother is a little unnerving." Julia said.

"Can't really imagine it," I said. I meant it, too. If Jake ever got bitten, I don't know if I could kill my brother, even a zombie brother.

We suddenly caught up to Jake, mostly because he had stopped moving. The path split at this point, the left hand side wandering off into a very dark, thickly wooded section of the path. The right hand side went up to the big bridge, and that was a dark maw that opened to the other side of the river. Looking up, I could see beams that I recognized as railroad ties, and that explained the size of this bridge. It had to be huge to handle the weight of the trains that once ran over it. When the bike path was built, it must have made sense to use the structure that was in place, rather than create a new one. For all the dumb things, we thought people did in the past; this one was actually pretty smart.

"Anyone want to go first?" Jake asked, grinning in the night.

"I'll do it," I said, stepping forward. I had never been afraid of dark spaces, even though there might be zombies. I could handle those if I needed to, and sometimes did. This bridge wasn't pitch black, but it was dark. On either side of me, there were openings that allowed me to see the river flowing past. The bridge was made of wood, and I could easily hear myself stepping across the old planks. My sword was held out in front of me at the low-ready position, with the thought that if there were a crawler on here that I couldn't see, it would get a bite at steel and not my leg.

At the first set of pylons, I stopped and looked at the river. It was very peaceful, and this would have been a nice place to live before things had ended. However, my reflections were interrupted by Julia bumping into my back and giggling.

"Keep going, doof," she said affectionately.

"Don't stop, dumbass," Jake added, not so affectionately.

"Quiet, the two of you," I replied, moving forward again.

At the second pylon, my sword bumped into something. I signaled to the others and they immediately went into ready positions. I explored what I hit with the tip of my sword, and figured out that whatever it was, it was about four feet long, and not moving. Reaching down carefully, I touched the obstruction and found it to be covered in fur.

Breathing a sigh of relief, I turned back to the other two. "Just an animal. Moving on." I stepped to the left and around the thing on the bridge, figuring it was someone else's problem to get rid of, not mine. Jake and Julia followed my steps, and as far as I could tell, no one tripped on Fuzzy.

CHAPTER 3

We reached the far side of the bridge without incident, and found ourselves in a small subdivision. There were small cottages along the river, and further to the west, there were some larger homes. Large trees lined the streets, and small fences separated the yards. I was sure that in the daylight this was a very beautiful place, one I might have only seen pictures in some of the books mom used to have.

We walked north, passing under the big tunnel that connected the north and south ends of the subdivision on either side of the tracks. The homes were quiet, the people either asleep or absent. I didn't see anything out of the ordinary, even thought we were looking for zombies. Jake, however, didn't miss much.

"Aaron, what's strange about these houses?" He asked.

I looked at the homes and didn't see anything really out of the ordinary. "I'm missing it. What is it?"

"The front doors are open on every other one on the river side," Jake said, pointing with his mace.

I'll be damned. He was right. It was like clockwork, and very, very weird. "I have a bad feeling about this," I said.

Julia nodded in the dark. "Me, too."

"We'd better have a look," Jake said.

"What are we looking for?" I asked, stepped over a small fence that blocked off the yard from the street.

"Something that might tell why there was an outbreak up here," Jake said. "They don't just happen on their own these days."

That was true. Actual accidental outbreaks were very rare, and we had found that recently someone was causing them deliberately. Why, we had no idea, but we knew we had to stop them for the simple reason we were the only ones around that could.

I reached the door and waved back the other two. "I got this. Just hang on."

Julia frowned but didn't say anything. I knew I might have to soothe some feelings later, but right now, I didn't have the time. I left my sword on my back, since it was almost useless inside a room that wasn't as big as a classroom.

I stepped through the door and looked around carefully. The house looked like it was lived in, but there wasn't any activity. I moved through the living room and looked into the kitchen. The place was neat and clean, so someone must at least take care of it. I carefully opened a cabinet and found canned food there, so I knew somebody had to call this place home.

I stepped back into the living room and moved towards the hallway that led to the bedrooms. At the nearest door, I looked in and saw a small form sleeping quietly on a bed. The little one was snoring softly and it was blissfully unaware of any danger.

I closed the door carefully and stepped across the hall towards the other bedroom. I felt a little weird, since I really had no real explanation as to why I was there, except for the fact the door was open. Someone could seriously take a shot at me and no one could blame them.

In the other room, things were very different. A man and woman lay on the bed, and both were breathing heavily. They were on their backs and covered in sweat. Their eyes stared blankly towards the ceiling, and didn't respond when I tapped carefully on the dresser with my tomahawk. I stepped closer, and then pulled out my small flashlight. I had a bad feeling about these two and needed to be sure.

Replacing the clear lens with a blue one, I shined the light carefully on the couple's faces. Their skin glowed yellow under the blue beam, a sure sign they were infected with the virus. I had very little time, as their breathing was slowing down, and soon they would slip away, their bodies reanimated by a virus that just refused to go away.

I pulled a length of cord out of my pack and tossed one end under the bed. Circling around, I pulled it up and stretched it across the pair's necks, effectively pinning them to the bed. I flipped it under the bed again, and this time stretched it across their stomachs, keeping their arms from rising up. As I finished, their breathing stopped. From this point, I had about an hour.

I ran outside and grabbed Jake and Julia. "We have a problem," I stated, and filled in the other two. They were shocked at first, but got serious enough when I mentioned the child. "We have to check the rest of the houses with the open doors. I have a feeling we'll see a lot more of this. "

Jake bared his teeth slightly, a sure sign he was pissed off. "We have to get the kids out if they're uninfected."

"Quit talking to me and move, then," I said. Jake threw me a look, and then was off down the street.

Turning back to Julia, I said, "Take care of yourself. I don't know what's in the rest of the houses, but chances are they're infected."

Julia nodded and was off like a wraith. I went back into the house and checked on the couple. Their eyes were still closed, so I used my tomahawk to send both over the divide fully. Once that was done, I went back to the other bedroom and carefully gathered up the small sleeping form into a snug bundle. The little guy, who couldn't have been older than three years, slept through the whole thing.

Leaving the house, I moved towards the next one with an open door, and waited until Jake came out. He was leading a teenage girl and a small boy, both of whom were trying to hold back tears. I spoke to the girl and got her to take the small bundle from me.

I motioned Jake to the side. "Same thing?"

"Looks like it. Both parents were infected and about to turn."

"Way too coincidental. You thinking what I'm thinking?"

"If you're thinking about Julia's ass, no, I'm not," Jake said casually.

I almost missed what he said, and when I had finally processed it, he was already off, heading towards the next house in the line. I bit off my retort, especially when I realized

I *was* actually thinking about Julia's rear end. Shaking my head, I went past the third house down the line just as Julia exited, carrying a small bundle. It was a little boy, no older than three months. I exhaled slowly, trying to contain my rising anger. If his parents had turned and found him, likely they would have consumed him entirely. Not a fun thing to think about.

CHAPTER 4

Julia looked up at me and frowned, and I was about to speak when Jake waved me over to the last house on the row. I ran over quickly, followed by Julia and a small collection of weepy, sleepy kids.

"What's up?" I asked, wondering what the trouble was.

"Need you to see something, then tell me what you think it means," Jake said.

"Lead on, old son," I said, gripping my weapons. I was actually looking forward to some kind of activity. My blood was up and it wasn't going to go well for any undead I might encounter in the near future.

Jake led me to the back bedroom, and there was a woman lying on her side. Her labored breathing filled the air with a promise of death, and I had to keep from slamming my tomahawk down on her temple that instant.

"Look by her collarbone," Jake said.

I leaned over, careful not to disturb her in any way. I looked her up and down, and didn't see anything unusual on the first pass. On the second, however, I saw what Jake wanted me to see. At the base of her neck, there was a circle of veins, black in color and fanning away from a central dot in an almost lazy pattern. I wasn't fooled. We'd seen enough infected flesh in our lives that we were almost immune to it. This woman hadn't been bitten. She had been deliberately infected with the virus.

I turned back to Jake and stepped aside as his mace descended down. It finished off the woman with a heavy crunch, and then Jake stepped to the side.

"Any ideas?" He asked.

"Well, the what is that she was infected, and the how is through a needle in her neck. The big questions are the who and the why," I said, looking out the bedroom window.

"Exactly. This wasn't a random outbreak, and it sure wasn't anyone messing around with one of the old zombies that got careless," Jake said.

"Well, what can we do...hang on." I stared intently, wishing like crazy it was light out. I thought I saw movement across the road, and I was hoping to have a clear vision of what it was.

As I stared out the window, I saw a subdivision across the street buried in darkness. The trees were very grown over there, blocking out any moonlight that might have made it to the ground, and since it was overcast, the darkness was almost tangible.

"There!" I jabbed a finger at the glass, and showed Jake what I had thought I had seen earlier. A man was leaving a home, jogging quickly across the street. He didn't look our way once, which was probably a good thing since we should have attracted attention with all of the castaways we had rounded up.

The man stopped at a home and squatted down by the front door. From our vantage point, we could see him working the door quickly and quietly. By his feet there looked to be a bag, but it was too hard to tell in the darkness what it really looked like.

In a few minutes, he had managed to open the door on the house and slipped quietly inside.

"Come on!" Jake said, turning and running for the open door.

I was right on his heels and stopped only briefly to tell Julia to head for the rest of the community and drop off the kids. I told her not to tell them what had happened until we could get this thing settled down. In the back of my mind, I was thinking about the rest the zombies we hadn't accounted for.

Jake was down the street and approaching the house when I showed up on the sidewalk. Jake was crouched low, swinging wide and coming up around the garage side of the house, trying to stay out of sight of the windows. I went over to the house the man had exited, walking through the open front door. This subdivision was larger than the other one and I found myself inside a split-level home. I checked the downstairs quickly and headed for the upstairs bedrooms. I was hoping whoever lived here didn't have any children.

A glance into the nearest rooms revealed a library and a workout room, so I reasoned whoever was in here probably didn't have kids. The last bedroom door was ajar and I made my way slowly, keeping my Ka-Bar knife out in front of me, my tomahawk held back and ready.

Pushing the door open slowly, I eased into the room. I was expecting to see another couple lying on the bed, quickly succumbing to the injected virus. What I got, however, was a naked woman lying on her stomach, her head buried under a couple of pillows. I flicked on my light, and she lit up as if she was infected, so that was that. As I approached to finish her off, I noticed a blemish on her left buttock. I shook my head as I figured out that whoever had broken in here, they had found a woman who slept in the nude, and injected her through her butt cheek. The humor of it escaped me as I pulled the pillows away to expose the back of her head. A quick punch with the knife and I was out the door again.

When I reached the front door, I heard a lot of grunts and sounds as if someone was hitting a bag of sand. I stepped outside and found Jake engaged in a serious fight with a man who clearly didn't want anyone to have found out what he was doing.

CHAPTER 5

Jake and the man circled each other, and I could see the man had some kind of training. He held his hands open, about level with his face. He kept his eyes on Jake, and I could make out a dark line by the corner of his mouth. It looked like Jake had scored at least one hit.

The man's eyes flicked over to me, and Jake took advantage of the opportunity to lash out with his left hand, striking the man's right forearm and knocking it into his face. The bigger distraction allowed Jake to step forward and land a blow to the man's midsection, eliciting a grunt and a roundhouse that missed by a mile.

The man jumped forward suddenly, shoving a right jab towards Jake's face. Jake slipped the punch and uppercut the man's arm, pushing it up and opening a chance to strike at the man's exposed ribs, which Jake did with a crack that I heard from across the street.

The man backed away, holding his side and staring hot murder at Jake, who stepped away from the clumsy punch that missed by a yard. Jake tried another punch at the man's head, but got his fist blocked and a return jab turned Jake's head an inch. The older man grinned and tried a duo of jabs, but Jake slapped them away and landed a punch on the man's nose that started another dark line to trickle down the man's angry face.

The man stepped back, shaking his head and wiping the blood off his nose. He reached into his bag, and Jake stepped away, his hand pulling out his knife as he got a good look at what the man was holding. From my position, I couldn't see anything, but it looked like it was a small knife or something.

Whatever it was, Jake was very cautious about it. He held out his knife in front of him, slowly sliding his feet forward, making sure his footing was secure. I wondered what the man was holding, and it suddenly dawned on me.

It was a syringe of zombie virus. One scratch from that evil thing, and Jake was a dead man. The other man thrust the needle towards Jake, and Jake jumped back, keeping his knife out. The man stepped forward, but stopped when Jake said something low that I couldn't hear. The man with the syringe moved back a couple of steps, keeping an eye on Jake and his knife.

It occurred to me that Jake had an infected knife, since that was what he must have used to kill the sleeping zombies. So the two men were facing off with deadly metal in their hands. In a strange way, I actually found the conflict ironic. However, the feeling lasted a fraction of a second and I ran over to the combatants, tomahawk at the ready. At this distance, I could easily plant the blade in the man's forehead without much trouble.

The man backed away, the prospect of facing two men too much, and he suddenly bolted for the side yard. I wasn't about to chase him down, so I let fly with my 'hawk. The weapon sailed across the grass, and the axe blade buried itself in the calf of the fleeing man. The man cried out and went down in a heap, pulling at the weapon that had brought him down.

I ran over with Jake right behind me. As we approached the man, he lunged at us, striking out with the virus. I danced back, bumping into Jake.

"Watch it, he's still got that syringe," I said, pulling out my falchion. With that needle around, I wanted to be able to do damage from a distance, and three feet of sharpened steel could do just that.

The man's eyes grew wide at the sight of my sword, and Jake pulled out his mace as well. The man saw that we could kill him without threat to ourselves, so he did the wise thing and dropped the syringe.

"Back up," I said, indicating movement with the sword.

"I can't! My leg is bleeding!" The man touched the tomahawk sticking out of his calf and hissed in pain.

I stepped close and kicked him in the chest, pushing him back several feet and dropping him to the ground. He cried out in pain and tried to sit up, but the point of my sword touched his throat and he stayed where he was. All I needed to do was lean forward two inches to kill him and he knew it.

Jake carefully retrieved the hypodermic and walked over to the man on the ground. He yanked the tomahawk out of the prone man's leg, earning a short bark of pain and a murderous glare from the recipient.

Squatting down, Jake wiped the blade of the axe on the man's shirt. Scared eyes followed Jake's moves and it was a full minute before Jake spoke.

When he did, it was right to the point. "Why are you turning people into zombies?" Jake asked, holding the syringe out over the man's face.

The man stared hard at the deadly thing above his face, and then swallowed. "I don't know what you're talking about. I live in this house. I just forgot my keys and had to break in. Why did you attack me when I came back outside?" The man tried to sound indignant, but it was tough when Jake laughed in his face.

"Really? You live here?" Jake chuckled. "So what's this then?" Jake waved the needle over the man and then placed his hand in a position to use it as intended. "Why did you try to poke me with it?"

"You were attacking me! I don't have any weapons! What was I supposed to do?"

I had to admit the man could make a convincing argument. However, we knew what he was up to, so it didn't matter. "Who sent you to do this?"

"I live here! No one sent me! Who the hell are you?" The man gave it his all, and I had to admire the arrogance of him.

"What's in the syringe?" Jake asked.

"Nothing bad. You can inject yourself and see." Scared eyes gave way to crafty ones, and it wasn't a pleasant sight.

Jake chuckled. "Here's the problem as I see it. You're not complaining enough, and you're not yelling for your neighbors to wake up and help you. When we fought, you were silent. In fact, you went out of your way to be quiet. So I'd guess if we woke up your neighbors, not a single one of them would know who you are. If the stuff in this needle is safe, we'll give you a little poke."

Jake stabbed down with the syringe, stopping just short of the man's chest when the killer screamed in terror. Jake pulled the needle away and the man's relief was almost tangible.

"Nothing bad, huh?" Jake asked. The man deflated, and refused to meet our eyes. The sky overhead was beginning to take on the early morning purple of sunrise, and I suddenly had a nearly overwhelming desire to go to sleep.

"Who sent you?" I asked again. I touched the tip of the sword to the man's throat, and he tried to burrow into the grass with the back of his head.

"I don't know! " The man said. "I just get a bag of coins, a metal box containing the needle, and the name of a town. That's it!"

"That's it? You go to cause outbreaks, death and destruction, and you have the nerve to say 'that's it'?" I was getting angrier by the minute. "I ought to kill you right now on general principles."

"Think you're so great?" The man sneered. "Why are you defending these sheep? A new world is coming and you can't do anything about it."

"I can," Jake said quietly. He placed the tip of the needle against the man's neck. Just enough to let him know it was there, but not enough to break skin. "I'll ask you one last time, and then I'm going to inject you with the 'not bad' stuff you wanted me to inject into myself."

"Aaaagh! Wait! No! I'll tell you what I know!" The man tried to twist away, but he didn't dare move too quickly. Any thrashing around his head and he was dead.

"Quickly, then. I get tired of games," Jake said.

"All I know is the leader of the group who wants to take over is named Ben. I don't know his last name. But I know he hates this world and he hates the man who made it happen," he said.

That didn't make any sense to me. "What are you talking about?" I asked.

"I heard the man who built society again is the same man Ben blames for his brother's death. I don't know any more!"

I looked over at Jake, and he was deep in thought. He shifted forward and started to ask a question. "Tell me something..."

Suddenly the man screamed and pulled away, scrambling to his feet and trying to hobble away. His leg kept giving out on him, and he kept falling to the ground, but he still got up repeatedly. I followed him with my sword, figuring to smack his legs and trip him up, but as I got closer, the man suddenly turned and lunged at me. I brought up my sword reflexively and he ran himself through. His face was a study in pure hatred, and he died cursing.

"Jesus, what the hell?" I asked, pulling my blade out of the man.

"Better give him one on the noggin, Aaron," Jake said.

"What? Why?" I asked, bringing up my blade.

"'Cause I accidentally poked him with the needle. Sorry." Jake was actually apologetic.

"Well, it would have been nice to get some more info, but we have a good start," I said.

"Not that good," Jake said. "We don't know where this man got his information and weapon from, or where this new threat is coming from."

I thought for a second. "I blame you," I said.

Jake gave me a lopsided grin as he picked up on of the man's hands and dragged him off the lawn.

"So do I, Aaron. So do I."

CHAPTER 6

We waited until the first vestiges of sunrise came creeping over the horizon, then we made our way over to the center of town. We still hadn't found the fifteen missing zombies, and that was cause for some concern, since all it took for a real mess to start was one of them. If all of them decided to drift off in different directions, we were going to be slightly busy. Add to the fun that a group was deliberately causing outbreaks, and I was seriously considering going back to bed and hiding under the covers.

We walked along the street that paralleled the river, and I was again surprised at how nice this little community was. If I were ever to leave the lodge, this would be a nice alternative.

I mentioned it to Jake, who nodded and then threw cold water on my dreams.

"Would suck if the river flooded," he said casually, looking at the water flowing by.

I had to resist the urge to throw him in the water. He did still have the syringe full of zombie virus. The plan was to take the virus back to the capital and see if there was anything extra special about the serum, or if it was just your standard, run of the mill zombie goop.

When we reached the main road, we turned east towards the town. There were a lot of businesses in that area, and it looked like many of them had made a kind of comeback. One restaurant even had a balcony, which reached out over the river.

A small dam ran the width of the river at this point, raising the north end about four feet. A power plant was located across the water at this point, and seemed to be managing the power needs of the small community. The sky was bluing up nicely as the sun regained its proper place, and I was looking forward to seeing Julia again.

Jake began crossing a stone bridge when he stopped suddenly. "I'll be damned."

"What?" I asked, trying to twist around to see what was the matter. I looked down and joined Jake in his personal religious assessment skills. "I'll be damned."

The business district had a series of deep ditches which captured overflow from the river and sent it out a massive storm drain. The ditches were brick lined and ran around the foundations of the buildings, allowing some bridges to add to the charm of the community. When the ditches were flooded, I'm sure it actually looked nice, although you probably couldn't hear yourself think out here when that drain was flowing. A huge aluminum grate kept out most large things from flowing away, while smaller stuff would go through easily. A ladder was located next to the grate, and a small, two-foot high fence kept the little ones out of the ditch.

That wasn't what had caught our attention. What had, was the mini-horde of zombies that milled about in general and groaned in particular. They must have wandered this way in the night, and tumbled as a group into the ditch. The fence was just high enough to hit the zombies in the knees and allow them to fall over the edge.

As we looked on, we could see several zombies that had managed to commit suicide by landing on their stupid heads. I glanced around, and although the zombies were right there for the killing, there wasn't any safe way to engage them.

"Any thoughts?" I asked. We could use the ladder, I supposed, but it had its own risks and I wasn't a fan of fighting on unstable ground.

Jake looked it over. "Well, we could...no. Um...we could...wait." Jake scowled at the zombies. "Huh."

I knew then he was as stumped as I was. There wasn't any way in hell I was going to jump in there, and we sure weren't going to let them out. If we had something long, we might be able to get away with it, but not right now.

"Hang on, I have an idea," Jake said as he jogged back the way we had come. I had nowhere to be right now, so it wasn't hard to remain true to the charge.

About ten minutes later, Jake came jogging back with a cinder block on his shoulder and a length of rope. He tied the rope to the cinder block, and then carefully lowered it until it was about three feet from the ground in the ditch. Several zombies touched and grabbed the block, but after they realized it wasn't anything to eat, they weren't interested.

Jake held the block down, and then tied the other end of the rope to the fence, making sure he kept the length the same. I watched curiously, since I wasn't sure where this was going.

When Jake had everything he needed ready, he pulled up the cinder block and looked over at me, holding the stone above his head.

"Got this idea from Dad's journal. You want to go first, or can I?" Jake asked.

I suddenly realized what he was talking about. "That's brilliant. You can go first, you thought of it." I leaned over the rail and watched as the hungry ghouls reached up in frustrated hunger at the food that they would never be able to reach.

Jake hurled the cinder block down, and it cracked the skull of a middle-aged man. As he went down, the rope went taut and kept the block from hitting the ground. Jake hauled up on the rope and handed the stone to me.

"Your turn." He said with a smile.

"This will take a while, methinks," I said, looking for a target. The rope limited our range, but that was okay, since the zombies always came to us, no matter what.

"I'm open to suggestions," Jake said testily.

I threw the block down, nailing a teen in the face as he looked up. His forehead flattened from the impact, and he fell over.

"I was thinking of holding you upside down while you smacked away with your mace," I said, pulling on the rope. A zombie took hold of it and hung on. I gave the rope a few quick jerks, and the zombie let go.

Jake didn't dignify that with an answer; he just took the block from me and killed another zombie.

We worked that crowd for about a half an hour, and managed to kill nearly all of them. The last one was tough, since he had to climb over the bodies of his comrades, and both Jake and I missed several times trying to nail him. Finally, on what seemed like the hundredth throw, Jake caught him perfectly on the top of the head with the cinder block, dropping that annoyance for good.

"All right, then. Let's get Julia and get out of here," I said. "We need to get that crap in the syringe to the government."

"Yeah, I'd hate to see what someone else might do with it," Jake said.

CHAPTER 7

We had a bit of a mystery on our hands. Someone was obviously trying to cause an outbreak, but the purpose behind it was unclear. Did they want to wipe out everyone, throw us back into the dark ages, living in caves and hoping the zombies don't find us? Granted it would be different this time, since there weren't as many people around to get infected, but in the last twenty years of relative peace and quiet, people have been doing a pretty good job of getting things running and rebuilding the population. There were a lot of kids around, and as I thought about it, I realized that if someone got a bunch of kids infected, we'd all be in trouble.

We moved towards the other side of town, heading towards the restaurant. It was the most easily defended place in town, and was a backup location in case of an outbreak. That much we had learned when we arrived here.

Jake retrieved the needle from its hiding place, and carefully carried it with him. I thought that having it out in the open was probably a bad idea, so as we walked, I looked for something we could store it in. I wanted to find something that was sealed, so in case the thing broke, the virus would be contained.

As we made our way to the holding area, we passed a small food store. I looked in, and saw they had a lot of canned goods on the shelves. That gave me an idea, so I went into the back room and found a number of jars and lids. Jake saw what I found and happily transferred the needle into the jar. I put the lid on, and then transferred the small jar to my pack. As I looked at the liquid in the light, I swear it swirled on its own. If I had put some on a counter, I firmly believe the evil stuff would have tried to make its way over to me. That's how creeped out I was over it. If I had to think about it, I was angry, too. I couldn't figure out how anyone could hate so much that they would be willing to kill the world. It didn't make any sense.

With the needle secured, we made our way to the river, and then the restaurant. Along the way, we burned off the remnants of the virus from the killings at the houses. As we did that, I started to get angry about the number of orphans that were needlessly created. Sure, someone would take them in, but why was it necessary? If someone hated the world that much, why cause suffering? Just suck a gun barrel and pull the trigger. All hate would be gone.

I said as much to Jake, and he nodded in agreement.

"It does seem like a lot of trouble to go through. If you wanted to start an outbreak, why bother with all the secretive stuff? Doesn't make any sense. There are still plenty of zombies in the cities. Just knock down a wall or two and wait for the fun to begin," Jake said.

"Makes you wonder why they are trying to do things this way," I replied.

"Well, if we can figure out the plan, we can get ahead and finish this before it does become a major outbreak."

"Good luck with that," I said.

"Why?"

"Right now we've got two small outbreaks which we handled. Taken together, they seem to be a part of a plan, but the communities are nowhere near each other. Right now, it's looking like just experimentation, with something else to hit us at another time."

"Think we're being tested?" Jake speculated.

"Not us. I think society is, and how it reacts will determine the next move by our mutual enemy," I said.

Jake looked at me sideways.

"What?" I asked, not liking his look.

"You sounded like dad just then."

I thought for a minute. "Not a bad thing, considering."

Jake looked off into the distance. "Wouldn't hurt to have the old man around right now," he said quietly.

"Yeah," I said, just as quietly.

At the restaurant, we made our way through a number of people who looked at us with anxious eyes. I found the leader of the community and quickly relayed what we had found and where they would need to send crews to get bodies out of houses. When they asked about how the outbreak started, I hesitated for a minute, but then realized they needed to be on alert, more so than they had been.

"It was a deliberate infection. Someone came and injected those poor people with the virus, trying to start a major outbreak up here," I said, bracing for the response.

I wasn't disappointed. Several gasps and many curses followed with a few questions being shouted, along with numerous threats.

I held up my hands for quiet as Julia worked her way forward from the back of the restaurant where she was entertaining some of the children.

"I don't have answers for you. I truly don't, but someone is trying to unmake everything that we've done over the past twenty years, and they don't seem to care how they go about it. We have a lead, and we're working on that, but for right now, you people need to be wary of strangers, keep your eyes open, and lock your doors at night. It would probably be a good time to pull out the weapons and start practicing again." As I said this, several older heads in the room nodded, and I knew they would be just fine. It was the younger ones I worried about.

"There's a bunch of turned folk down in the ditch, so someone will need to get them out. You guys will be fine, just keep on your toes, and listen to your veterans," I said as I moved towards the door. Julia was right behind me and I had a feeling she had questions. Jake was at the door, but as I finished he slipped out.

I was right behind him and Julia took my hand in hers. I gave her a smile and she winked at me, making me feel a whole lot better after having spent the night chasing zombies and getting absolutely no sleep whatsoever.

"What's the next move, Jake?" I asked as my brother made his way back to the truck.

"We need to get that syringe to the capital, and see if we can't get a meeting with the president." Jake said.

"What for?" Julia asked, beating me to the punch.

Jake stopped and turned around. "In case you hadn't noticed, there are just three of us. What if there's a large outbreak that we can't control? What then? We can't throw rocks at all of them."

It made sense, and we were very lucky so far in that we had been able to contain the infections we had come across so far. But if that zombie party hadn't fallen in that ditch, we'd probably still be fighting.

"All right, let's get it going then," I said. "But I'll likely sleep on the way, so one of you drive."

Jake shook his head. "I stopped sleeping a while ago, so I got this."

CHAPTER 8

We reached the truck and I let Julia stretch out in the back while I made myself as comfortable as possible. We only had a three-hour drive to the capital, so I needed to make the most of it. Jake was silent as we drove, which helped, and Julia was out cold, so that helped even more. As I drifted off in the morning sun, I couldn't help but think briefly about why we were the ones chasing ghosts and not leaving it up to others.

The next thing I knew, I was being awakened by my brother opening the door I was sleeping against. I grabbed the nearest thing to me to stop my fall. Unfortunately, for Jake, that happened to be his collar, and I ended up yanking him down to the ground on top of me.

"Oof!"

"Ouch! My neck, you stupid fool! Hey! Quit..." Jake's verbal harangue ceased when my hand that was clutching his collar inched up and fastened itself on his neck.

I tossed Jake off of me to see a grinning Julia standing there refreshed and lovely.

"Little help?" I asked, holding up a hand.

"Of course, sweetie." Julia grabbed my hand and heaved me to my feet. She was remarkably strong for her size, something easily forgotten until it was used against you.

Finally upright, we pulled Jake to his proper vertical position and I held up a warning hand to his angry stare.

"You choose to open a door I was sleeping against. Am I responsible for your actions?" I asked, holding his gaze.

Jake was wrestling internally with agreeing with me or punching me. I knew what he chose when he shook his head and turned on his heels. We walked quickly through the streets of Leport, winding our way towards the presidential residence.

Despite the name, it was simply a modest Victorian home, nestled within the confines of a hillside community. Our father originally chose the place, saying that the president should not live in a palace, or reside anywhere that the people who elected him could not stop by on occasion to just chat. The presidents, and there had been three since our father had been one, all agreed to the duty to the people, and hadn't changed anything since.

The house was a two-story affair, with a porch wrapping around most of the first floor. As we approached, we saw a middle aged man sitting in a rocker on a corner of the porch, taking in the morning and breathing in the river air.

"Hello the house!" Jake called. It was a courtesy of the times to announce yourself if possible.

"Hello, yourself! Come on up and join me," a deep voice responded.

We made our way to the porch, passing by some very nice gardens and flowerbeds. Julia stopped to smell a rose, but Jake was focused on the man on the porch, who stood at the top of the stairs awaiting our arrival. At the far corner of the porch, another man sat with a rifle across his knees. The pose was casual, if you ignored the fact his hand was on the rifle's grip and his finger was inside the trigger guard. At the first sign of trouble, that gun could kill us before we had a chance even to react. I thought it was a nice touch, but I could see Jake throw a few glances that way.

The man who greeted us was tall, and the years hadn't stooped him a bit. He was about mid-forties, I'd guess, but that didn't seem to bother him. He was lean, with quick eyes, and the demeanor of someone used to command. His hair was blond turning to white, and he looked us up and down as we approached. He looked the longest at Jake, and I got the feeling he knew who we were.

"Welcome! How can I be of service to you?" The President said. "Please, sit down."

We positioned ourselves around the table, and at that moment, the guard materialized at the president's shoulder.

"Sir? These people are armed. Shall I gather their weapons?" The man said. The rifle was held low and out of the way, but he was fooling no one. One flick of the wrist and a squeeze of the finger and someone was going to get blasted.

The president looked at us and smiled. "I don't think so. These folks are the kids of friends of mine, and unless I seriously miss my guess, they don't mean to harm anyone they don't have to." The president looked at my brother. "Right, Jake?"

CHAPTER 9

Jake started a bit. I imagine the last thing he expected was for the President of the New United States to know who he was. For that matter, I think I was a bit startled myself. Julia looked quizzically at the exchange, and I hoped she wouldn't do anything silly.

The president smiled. "Allow me to fully introduce myself. I'm Trevor Jackson, formerly Captain Jackson of the Montana Minutemen, and formerly a friend of your father. I knew you when you were just a babe, Jake, and I was with your father during the Zombie Wars." President Jackson looked at Julia. "I knew your father as well, young lady, and have the honor of calling him my friend.

"Now that's me. However, I don't think we've met, young sir." President Jackson looked right at me, and extended his hand. His grip was strong, and while his smile reached his eyes, something was behind them that made you cautious.

I had read about Trevor Jackson in my father's book. From the very beginning of the end of the world, Jackson was leading men, fighting zombies, and venturing into some very remote territory. When he was just about my age, my father sent him into the wilds to learn about what might have happened to the centers the state had set up. What he found out was not pleasant at all.

"I'm Aaron, sir. Nice to meet you." I matched his grip, and hoped he would be friendly about it.

"Well met, Aaron. I knew your mother. How are your parents, by the way? I haven't seen them in a while.' The president asked.

Julia spoke up while Jake and I remained silent. "Our mothers are dead, President Jackson. They were helping with the cholera outbreak in Ottawa when they both got sick. They died within three days of each other."

Jackson looked down. "I'm sorry. Such a tragic thing. To have survived the zombies only to be taken out by a disease that once was curable. Very sad. What about your fathers?"

Julia shrugged. "After the funeral, our dads kept to themselves for a while, then just up and left. They left a note and told us not to follow. They'd be back after a while."

President Jackson looked thoughtful. "So as far as you know, they're still alive?"

Jake spoke up. "No idea, actually. But they're unavailable, so we're picking up the slack, as it were."

Jackson looked hard at Jake. "At least you have slack, son. You might figure on a little gratitude when he returns."

Jake returned the stare. "If he does, and I'm not so sure I'd welcome him if he did."

"You will." The President looked very confident, and I found myself believing it, even though I knew the odds were long. If Dad could return, why didn't he?

"So, with introductions out of the way, what can I do for you?" The president sat back in his chair, and waited patiently.

"Well, sir, our problem begins with this." Jake pulled out the canning jar that held the syringe. In the noon light, it was still as dark and nasty as we had seen it previously.

The guard stepped forward, but retreated as the president raised his hand. "Interesting. What is it?" he asked as he studied the needle

"We took that off of a man in St. Charles. He was breaking into homes as people slept and injecting them with it," Jake said.

"What? Why? What's in it?" Jackson did not look as closely as he had before.

"It was turning people into zombies. Our guess is that you're looking at a syringe full of straight Enillo Virus," I said.

The president sat back in his chair. "Holy Mother of God."

CHAPTER 10

I understood how he felt. He was looking at death incarnate right on his own front porch. The slightest prick from that needle and you were dead and gone, reanimated later as a carnivorous corpse. If someone put that mess into an aerosol spray, a room full of people could be infected at once. The guard stepped back a pace as well, and in that minute I got a good look at the man. He was as old as the president himself, with years of hard fighting etched into the lines of his face. I suddenly realized this was one of the original men that Trevor Jackson had started out with, fighting side by side for years. Now, he was still serving, as a loyal guard and companion, ending his years of service with honor.

President Jackson regained his composure quickly enough. "You said they were turning people into zombies. Do you know why? What happened to the man who owned this?"

Jake spoke up. "We don't know the why, and as to the man, he died from an injection of that same material. What we do know is there is a man behind this madness, someone called Ben, who seems to have a kind of vendetta against my father," Jake also relayed the information about the town that had been turned, and what we had done to contain it.

The President pondered that for a moment, looking off into the distance, but not really looking at anything. After a long pause, he shrugged. "Can't say as that brings anyone to mind, although your dad did make his share of enemies along the way." He turned his attention back to the jar. "What were you planning on doing with this?"

It was Jake's turn to shrug. "I figured we'd hand it over to the labs here at the capital and see if they had anything to say about it." Jake looked over at Julia and me. "After that, we're not really sure about doing anything but heading home."

"Well, let's talk about that. I'm actually very glad to see you three are here and seem to be well equipped to deal with this new crisis. Tell me, what have you been doing with yourselves for the last three years or so?" President Jackson asked.

Julia fielded that one. "We've been collectors. Going after the stuff people left behind."

"Really? And have you been to the city?" Jackson asked, leaning forward. Even his guard seemed very curious.

Julia nodded. "We've been there a few times."

"How many, could you remember?"

Julia looked at Jake and me. "I don't know, maybe a dozen, certainly no more than fifteen or sixteen."

We both nodded, remembering about the same number. I didn't see the significance, but I kept my mouth shut.

"Let me get this straight. You've successfully infiltrated the city, where the last known number of zombies was somewhere in the millions, collected what you needed, and made it out again at least a dozen times that you remember?"

"That's right."

President Jackson leaned back and shook his head. He looked over his shoulder at his guard and said, "I'd say they were qualified, wouldn't you?"

The guard simply nodded. There was something new in his eyes, something that looked almost like respect.

"What's the big deal?" Julia asked. "Lots of collectors go into the city."

The president chuckled. "Yes, they do, and the average number of trips survived is three. Your little band has beaten that number five times over. That's a big deal, little lady. Here's the thing, and hear me out. When the end came, most people died not because they were stupid or couldn't figure out how to survive. They died because they couldn't come to grips with what was right in front of them. They'd seen zombie movies and read zombie books, but the reality really did them in. Those that survived, like your fathers and me, took a simpler approach. Zombies were out to kill us and we didn't want to die. We found others like us and here we are today. Trouble is that people like myself and your fathers did our jobs too well. We took the fight to the zombies and either killed or contained them. People picked up their lives and started over, too willing to forget that the danger was out there, and could return.

"A lot of people my age, we could handle an outbreak. Trouble is, there aren't that many of us concentrated in a single area any more. We took our skills and branched out. We brought up our kids to fight and protect themselves, but that was more to the laws of nature and having the law too far away to do any good if we needed them. The rest of the people don't know of the world we once had, or how to handle a serious zombie outbreak. Hell, the army we have now is a bunch of kids that would likely wet their pants if a real zombie horde showed up."

"Which brings you to us and our current situation," Jake said.

"Exactly. You were trained for this, no question about it. You were trained to assess, analyze, and attack. You could do what an army couldn't. You can face the hordes and not flinch. If what you tell me is true, we've got some serious trouble coming our way." President Jackson looked over his shoulder and nodded at the guard, who promptly went into the house.

"What do you want us to do?" I asked.

"I need you to buy the capital some time. I don't have the men I need here to do the job that needs to be done. They're scattered all over, but they'll come if I call them. Right now, though, you're the best suited for the problem." The president looked at each of us. "Will you protect us?"

CHAPTER 11

Well, when he put it that way, I figured we didn't have a whole lot of choice, but to accept. I can't imagine even Jake in his darkest hours would refuse a request like that. Julia nodded right away, a small fire burning in her eyes. I nodded second, and Jake was right behind me.

"Good! You have the thanks of the President, and that will get you a drink somewhere, I'm sure. Take this." He scribbled a note on a piece of paper. "And bring it to the medical center. They'll take that piece of evil off of your hands and get an analysis running. And this," the president wrote another note. "Take this to the armory and get what you need."

President Jackson stood up and shook our hands. We left the porch feeling pretty good, and headed towards the medical center. It was a big building on the outskirts of town, and was probably better equipped than most hospitals from the old days. State of the art equipment had been moved here, and the lab was second to none. It was where we needed to go.

On the way, Jake spoke up. "Well, I have to say that little speech made more sense than just about any other explanation."

I had to agree. "Yeah, at least we have a kind of purpose, but I can't help but wonder what we do now? Do we go home, waiting for another outbreak? Do we drive around, hoping to head one off? I didn't see an answer for that in the speech."

Julia held my hand and gave it a squeeze. "Don't be silly. We'll stay the night, check over some maps, and figure out where the next attack might be. Easy."

Jake and I looked over her head at each other. Easy wasn't a thing that came to us very often.

We walked in silence over to the medical facility, and it was a rather simple looking building. A lot of effort had gone into making the place look as unimposing as possible, but everyone knew there was strange stuff going on in that place. All of the rumors could fill a large book if someone bothered to write them all down. I had heard they were working on making the zombies smarter and able to be trained. Another rumor went that there was some success in making the zombies not hungry any more. The best to me was the rumor that they were combining the Enillo Virus with DNA to create a person who never died.

All of it was crap, of course. The truth was that the place was where they worked on diseases as they had always done, finding cures for things and reviving cures for others. When the end had come, a lot of very smart people suddenly had become very dumb zombies. The pickup over the years had been slow, but the knowledge from previous years had thankfully been saved and restored. There were accidents and the like, but nothing serious.

The outside of the building was a simple white washed affair, with a single floor that ran well over three acres. The place had once been an envelope factory, but it now saw better days.

At the front, a single person greeted us at the main desk. She was a young brunette with big dimples, and Julia made sure to have a grip on my hand as we walked in. It didn't really matter, since the girl only had eyes for Jake.

"How may I help you?" She asked in a sweet voice.

"Hi, I need to speak to one of your Enillo researchers, please?" Jake asked. He handed the note over to the girl, who read it quickly. Her expression went from innocent to serious in a heartbeat, and she was on the phone during the second heartbeat.

"Jerry? It's Samantha. Drop everything and get up here, now." Samantha put the phone down and smiled again at Jake. "What are we going to help you with?"

Jake pulled out the canning jar and placed it on the desk. The lights of the office gave the liquid a purple cast, but it was a deep, malignant purple, the kind you'd use to decorate a lair for something wicked.

"Huh. And what might that be?" Samantha asked. She looked suspicious, since it wasn't every day that someone showed up with a note from the president and a jar with a syringe in it.

Jake smiled. "Let's let Jerry get here, that way, I don't have to repeat myself."

Samantha shrugged and looked over at me, but I just gave a half smile. It made sense, so we would just stand here in an uncomfortable silence until this Jerry, whoever he was, decided to make an appearance.

Julia rubbed my back, and I gave her a small hug which pulled her into me. We must have looked like a weird couple. I was over six feet tall, weighing in easily at two hundred and twenty pounds, most of which was packed on my chest and arms. Julia was petite and small, disappearing into my bulk.

A minute later, a short fat man rolled his way into the reception area. He was about five feet tall, with stubble on his chin and on his head. I think his beard was longer than his hair. He was wearing a lab coat and glasses, and looked to be somewhat put out to be summoned as he was.

"Hello. I'm Jerry Grossman, Chief Virologist and head of this facility. What can I do for you?" He extended a hand which Jake dutifully shook.

"Well, Jerry, you can take this," Jake handed him the note from the President, "and this." Jake handed the man the Mason jar.

Dr. Grossman looked the note over, his eyes widening a little. He then looked at the syringe. "What is it?"

Jake took a deep breath, and stepped back a space. I did the same and shielded Julia.

"We're pretty sure that's a syringe full of Enillo Virus."

"*Jesus!*" Dr. Grossman nearly dropped the jar in his haste to put it back on Samantha's desk, who clearly did not want to be anywhere near it. "Get the team up here now, full bio gear, move it!" Jerry stepped further away, wiping his hands furiously on his jacket.

Things got interesting after that. We stepped back into the shadows as several men in white hazard suits came running in. They took the Mason jar with its deadly cargo, placed it in a fish tank like container on wheels, and carefully whisked it away. Dr. Grossman wiped his forehead and came over to us.

"You could have warned me," he admonished us.

Jake smiled. "And miss the fun? No way. Besides, we could all be wrong and that's just grape preserves stuffed in that syringe."

Dr. Grossman laughed. "With my luck, that's what it will be. Where are you staying? Are you staying in town?" He changed the subject.

"We'll be here for a couple of days. We need to make a few stops and get some supplies. We also need to figure a few things out as well."

"Okay, well, I'll leave a note up here for you in a couple of days if you want to bring it to the president yourselves."

"Thanks, we appreciate that." Jake shook the man's hand and we headed back out into the capitol.

CHAPTER 12

A short walk towards the main part of town and we found ourselves in front of a restaurant. Julia gripped my hand tightly and I took that as a sign we needed to get ourselves fed. I was feeling a bit peckish, myself, now that I thought about it.

Inside the restaurant, a few people looked our way, but no one really gave us too much eyeballing. The waitress was friendly and in a short time, we were eating some really good sandwiches.

"So what's our next move?" I asked Jake around a mouthful of bacon, lettuce, and tomato.

"I'm thinking we hunker down around here and see what might be in that vial. After that I'm afraid we have nothing else to do but wait for the next outbreak." Jake said, munching on a pickle.

"That seems so strange," Julia said. "We have to wait for some idiot to go and cause death, rush to fight it, and hope we can find some clues to take us to the source."

When she put it that way, I had to admit it didn't make much sense. However, I really couldn't think of an alternative, and said so.

"What choice do we have? If someone out there is causing infections, the only thing we can do is put out the fires, map the outbreak, and triangulate on the source. Can't do that if we don't wait for them to happen. No one around here is going to know what's going on and there would be panic if they did," I said.

Sometimes, I think I have a gift for trouble. Every time I open my stupid mouth, exactly what I was talking about seems to happen. I was just finishing my sandwich when a teenage boy poked his head into the restaurant, spied us, and ran over to the table.

"Jake! Aaron! Julia! The president needs to see you right now!" The boy panted.

"All right, son, catch your breath, we're coming," Jake said, standing up, his hands automatically doing a quick check of his weapons.

I did the same and Julia put a couple of coins on the table to pay for our meal. We left the restaurant and followed the boy back to the president's home. President Jackson was on the porch, talking into a phone.

We waited a respectful distance away, but even at that range, we could hear words like "Okay, how many? When do you think it happened? Okay, I'm sending someone up right now."

The president hung up and waved us over. He had a map in front of him, and we could see he had drawn circles

"No time to waste. There's been an outbreak in Freeport. I need you up there now." President Jackson didn't waste time with pleasantries.

"On our way. We'll hit the armory and be gone within the hour," I said.

"Did you drop off the syringe?" Jackson asked.

"We did. Freaked out a few people over there." I chuckled at the memory.

"No doubt. They'll send their report to me and I'll let you know when I see you again. Stop at these three towns on your way to Freeport." He indicated the towns on the map. "Go to their comm centers and if I have a message for you, it'll be there."

Jake nodded. "We're gone."

We moved quickly back through the city. I wanted to head over to the armory but Jake said no.

"Why the hell not?" I asked, perturbed.

"You want to just take what we can carry, or would you like to back the truck up and load it there?" Julia asked.

I felt stupid. "Okay, let's get the truck."

We retrieved our vehicle and made our way to the armory. A centrally located building that had a small office in the front, and a big warehouse in the back. If rumors were true, there was some serious firepower in there. One quarter of the warehouse was devoted to making ammo, and there were people whose job it was just to crank out round after round after round. No one knew why we needed to keep making bullets, but we did.

The man behind the desk was a pleasant, middle-aged man who took our note from the president in stride. Apparently, we weren't the only ones who were given access by the chief executive.

We told the man what we wanted, and in a short amount of time, we had over three thousand handgun rounds sitting in the bed of our truck. A thousand rifle rounds joined in, and we were as good to go as we ever were.

"You guys want automatic weapons? You're authorized for them." The man raised a quizzical eyebrow.

Jake looked at me and I shook my head. He turned back to the man. "We're good. Besides, if things get bad for us, you're going to needing them more than we are."

We left the man with his mouth open, and boarded the truck. We had a good trip ahead of us, and I hoped we wouldn't be too late. It was a hundred mile trip to Freeport, and under the best conditions, it would take us about an hour and half. Under present conditions, it would take us about three hours. We stopped at a communication center and had a message relayed to our aunts and uncles about what we were doing, and a request to look in on the lodge for us.

"Let's get this rolling," Jake said.

"Question for you," I said as we pulled out of the capital and headed north to pick up the highway.

"Go for it."

"Ever miss being a collector?"

"Only lately, old son. Only lately."

CHAPTER 13

We stopped at two of the towns the president had mentioned, but we didn't have any news. At the third town, there was a message that another outbreak had occurred in the town of Homer Glen. We were too far to do anything about it, so we sent a message to our cousins Trey and Kayla, and asked them to look at things for us. They had been trained, as we had been, their parents having spent years fighting alongside ours. If there was anyone out there we could trust to have our backs in a fight, it was those two. Trey was Uncle Tommy's son, and he was a dead shot with rifle or pistol. His favorite mêlée weapon was a curved piece of metal about three feet long with a small wedge welded to the end. The last sixteen inches of the metal was sharpened, and it could take your leg off at the knee. Kayla was Uncle Duncan and Aunt Janna's daughter, and she was a blonde knockout. She was also lethal with any bladed weapon, be it a knife, sword, or pair of scissors. It didn't help she was a constant flirt, and several would-be boyfriends found themselves staring at the business end of something pointy when they tried to push their luck. They'd come with us on a couple of collections, but never got into it as seriously as we had.

I hoped as we travelled north that there wouldn't be any more outbreaks. I didn't know anyone else to send.

Julia interrupted my thoughts with an interesting question. "If there are enough outbreaks, do you think our dads will come back?"

I didn't have an answer to that one, but I secretly hoped it could be the catalyst.

CHAPTER14

"Move, move!"

"Jesus, where the hell did these guys come from?"

"Just move your ass!"

"There's nowhere to go, we're blocked!"

"Son of a bitch!"

"Save it and fight!"

I whipped my tomahawk up and jammed the pointed end into the temple of a zombie that had gotten past my pile of corpses. My sword was stuck in the head of a zombie that was quickly becoming buried in a pile of corpses, and I had nothing left but my knife and tomahawk. I had my gun, but that was for dire emergencies and I didn't want the horde to get bigger when other zombies heard the shots.

Suddenly, I heard a snap and the air filled with gunfire. The reports echoed off the buildings and came back to hurt my ears again. I turned my head just as seven zombies fell to the ground, each one wearing a hole in their foreheads.

"Follow!" Jake shouted. He jumped through the gap that had suddenly opened up and raced down the street.

I wasn't about to argue so I dove after him, figuring I would retrieve my sword later. Right now, I had more important things to worry about, such as saving my neck. I caught up to Jake as we ran from the zombies.

"Nice shooting, by the way," I said as I jogged next to him.

Jake suddenly stopped, and I skidded to a halt a few feet in front of him.

"What?" I asked, looking over his shoulder at the advancing horde of Freeport zombies.

"Aaron, I thought you shot them. I didn't." Jake looked at me funny.

I shook the surprise out of myself and grabbed Jake's arm. "Let's get the hell out of here. Whoever it was just did us a big favor. I'm not about to ask that gift horse to open wide." I ran down the street, trying to get some distance between us and the zombies, and while I was moving, I was thinking. Who shot those zombies? There wasn't anyone up here but the three of us, and right now I hope Julia wasn't in as much trouble as we were.

We turned down West Main Street and headed east. I knew the river was somewhere nearby, and where the river was, there were bridges. At least with a bridge we could hold them at a choke point, and not worry about something coming at us from another direction. Of course, it would be easier to hold them with my sword, but I wasn't going to say that out loud to Jake.

Some of the homes we ran past still had people in them, but they were wisely on the second floor, watching us run by. I had to think they didn't have too much confidence in us if we were running away. However, I had a plan, and hopefully, it would be a good one.

"They're still following us, Aaron," Jake said.

I slowed to a walk. "Good. I want to draw as many as I can behind us."

Jake looked back. The zombies were moving slowly, but they were moving, and since they were new zombies, they were faster with their feet than your average dead. Some of them were nice and clean, others had bloody gashes and bite marks on them. The clean ones had been deliberately infected, while the bloody ones had been unfortunate enough to run into the ones who had been injected. The whole situation was a mess, and every time I had to kill a zombie that didn't need to have been a zombie, I was mad about it.

Someone named Ben was behind an effort to start the zombie apocalypse all over again. We had intercepted a couple of his outbreaks, but it seemed like they were getting worse. This mess in Freeport was a prime example. By the time we got up here there had to be at least a hundred people infected, and since the town barely had over five hundred people living here, that was a significant chunk of the populace.

We walked past a hotel, and started our way through the downtown area. There was a movie theater up a side street, and I lost my train of thought when I realized I had never been to a movie. I had heard about them and read about them, but never had been to one.

I could see the river so I pulled my sidearm and fired two shots at the zombies. I hit one of them, and caused a few more to trip, but I had no idea where my second bullet went.

"What are you doing?" Jake asked.

"I told Julia we'd be heading this way, and I'd fire two shots to let her know we were coming. She should have the rest of the town in the right place by now," I said.

"Ah." Jake's reply was as concise as it was elegant.

When we had arrived, we had looked at the map and decided the best thing to do was to wander around as bait and try and collect the horde into one mass that could be dealt with at the same time. We killed the loners and the small groups, but as the numbers got bigger, we fell back to the plan, which was to get the groups into one horde and get them in a place where we could kill them at leisure. That was Julia's job.

At the river, we turned left and waited for the horde to catch up. They tried their best, they really did, but there was no way a meal was going to happen for them. I just didn't feel like being lunch today.

Jake spoke up as we turned. "Very nice. She did well."

Since a compliment from Jake was about as rare as a zombie who could whistle, I had to figure he approved. On the bridge, in the middle of the road, were three flatbed trailers for semi-trucks. Julia must have insisted on some sort of platform, and the townspeople had delivered marvelously. Standing on one of the trailers, I could see a small blonde holding a spear, waving as we came down the road.

Behind us, the zombies lurched and slouched, dipped and bobbed as they moved as best they could. There were about seventy-five of them, and they made an awful noise as they groaned and snarled and screeched at us. When they saw the buffet tables on the bridge, they made even more noise.

CHAPTER 15

We jogged the last few yards to the trailers, and I climbed aboard the middle one while Jake took the last one. I gave Julia a smile and a thumbs up as I went past, and she dimpled at me.

I addressed the people on the middle trailer, although I made my voice loud enough to be heard on the other two.

"Keep your feet back from the edge, and use your weapons wisely. Stabbing them will take less effort than smashing their heads in." Most of the people were armed with some sort of long weapon. A couple had just knives tied to long poles. "I know these are people you know. Keep in mind they aren't that person any more. That person died and their body is just being used by the virus to try and make another host. That's all they are. If you get sympathetic, you get dead."

I had nothing to say after that, since the zombies were upon us. They surrounded the first vehicle, and then several drifted off to the second vehicle, and so one. Soon we were all surrounded, and were busy dealing with the dead. The trailers were tall enough, but some were able to climb up a little on the tires and reach much further. I took care of those on my flatbed while the rest of the people poked and smashed the rest. I was really missing my sword after a just a few minutes of fighting. We had to be on our toes, though, because the more we killed, the higher the zombies could climb.

One managed to get up on the trailer, and I kicked him off rather than kill him up here, just because there wasn't enough room. A quick glance told me that the other trailers were having some of the same issues we were having.

The good news was we were winning. After a few minutes, the zombies had thinned out considerably; enough that Jake jumped off the back trailer and started dealing with the few that were not easily getting killed by the men on the flatbeds.

I followed his lead, slipping a little on one of the fully dead corpses ringing the trailer. Two zombies came at me and I adjusted my grip on my knife and my axe as I waited for them to come closer. The first one, a man about my brother's age and just as ugly, fell under my 'hawk as he came close. The second one tried to slip past the first, but I managed to turn quick enough to toss the dead zombie in front her. She was a slender, pretty teenager, and would have turned many a young man's head if it weren't for the fact she was missing half her face. Her shirt was a mess of blood and gore, and I wasn't sure how much was hers and how much might have been someone else's.

It didn't matter in the end. As she struggled under the weight of her dead comrade, I came around and stepped on her chest. She hissed up at me and tried to take a bite out of my shoe. I wasn't appreciative of her efforts, and drove my knife through her eye and into her skull in order to finish things.

Julia split the skull of the last one to attack her position, and in the brief silence that usually followed a good deal of fighting, I took a chance to look around. There wasn't any activity I could see, and for a change, I was optimistic we could get this job done.

Jake brought me out of my scouting by pointing to a hill. As I looked, I was struck by the sight before me.

"Son of a bitch," I said as I watched the figure walk slowly down the street. He was a young man, although a few years older than Jake. He was broad shouldered but lean, and dressed completely in black. His shirt was tucked into his cargo pants, held in place with a black belt sporting a silver buckle. I knew a Glock was on his hip, and I could see the several magazines that covered his left side. Dark sunglasses covered his face, but his blond hair was long and held back into a ponytail.

He looked like something out of a comic book, and he was carrying my sword. It was resting on his shoulder, and I wondered briefly, what I would have to do to get it back.

While he approached, I took the time to clean off my weapons and put them back in their sheaths. When I finished, he was close enough and both Jake and I went out to meet him.

Jake stopped in front of the man and looked him over before greeting him. "Hey, Logan. I guess those were your shots that made that hole for us," Jake said.

"Thanks," I added.

Our cousin, Logan Talon, paused to spit before he answered. "Heard you three were up this way, thought I'd see what you were doing. Good thing I did. Here's your butter knife, Aaron." Logan tossed my sword to me and I caught it out of the air. I didn't bother to sheath it, since I hadn't cleaned it.

"Thanks, Logan, you're too kind," I said. I didn't particularly like our cousin, he was a bit too standoffish and nasty for me, but since he was our dad's nephew, I cut him some slack. It didn't hurt he was a dead shot with any firearm. Dad had said he got that from his father. We'd had a brief fight before, and we both knew who would win. Away from his guns, Logan wasn't much good as a close quarters kind of guy.

That memory triggered another, and I spoke up in the brief but uncomfortable silence that followed the last words. "By the way, since we have you here..." I pulled out the Beretta at my hip and held it out to Logan. "Here you go."

Logan didn't move. "In case you got zombie goop in your eyes, I have a gun, and it just saved your ass. No thanks."

I persisted. "You want this one, I'm sure."

"No, I don't, *I'm* sure. Knock it off."

"It was your father's," I said, trying really hard not to say what was on my mind.

That changed things. Logan reached out and took the gun from me, holding in both hands near his chest. He looked at it for a long time before he spoke.

"How did you...How do you know...?" The questions didn't come out completely, but I knew what he wanted to know.

"My dad left it for me, along with a journal of everything he had done up to the point where he stopped the invasion of the zombie kids. Your dad died saving all of us from becoming part of them. Your mom took you away before he could give it to you, and not knowing what else to do with it, he gave it to me," I said kindly.

Logan just stared, and I wondered what was going on in his head. To give him some more room, I said, "That's the gun he used to get you and your sister out of the city, and the one he used to keep you safe as he took you to Starved Rock."

Logan held onto the gun, and turned around. Over his shoulder, he called out.

"Thanks. I'll be seeing you."

Jake watched him go. "Wonder why he hates us?"

I shook my head. "I think he just hates me."

Julia came up behind me and put her arm around my waist. "Everything okay with Logan?"

I shrugged. "It's the same. Let's get these corpses out of here and get moving. God knows where another outbreak might occur in the next ten minutes."

CHAPTER 16

We used the flatbeds to haul the bodies away. It was convenient as hell to just toss them up and roll them away. I'd have to remember that one.

Returning to our truck, we did a quick tour of the city and found that there were a few more zombies that were just now coming out of their homes. I was about to stop and deal with them when Jake called out.

"Keep going, faster! Get to the end of the block!" He yelled.

I gunned the engine and fairly flew down the street, but it was hard because I didn't know what I was chasing or running from.

"Turn left!" Jake pointed and started scrambling in the back seat for a gun.

"Hey! Watch it!" Julie protested Jake's rummaging.

"Give me the carbine, dammit!" Jake cursed.

"Here, you jerk!" Julia shoved the gun in his face. I was very uncomfortable with the fact the muzzle was behind my ear when she did that.

"See that car going away?" Jake asked as he rolled down the window

"Yeah?"

"Get close. I think they're the ones who were spreading the virus," Jake said, sitting out on the edge of the window.

"How do you know?" I shouted, the roar of the engine loud in the cab.

"I saw them run out of a house. If they try to run, they're guilty," Jake said, shouldering his weapon.

Julia spoke up from the back seat. "Maybe, they're running because a big black truck is chasing them."

"Shut up, will you?" Jake said.

I swerved a little and he shifted enough to grab onto the handle above the door inside the cab.

"All right! Sorry! Try not to kill me, Aaron." Jake's apology sounded sincere given the fact I was ready to dump his ass if he was rude to Julia again.

Julia, for her part, put a hand over the seat and rubbed my shoulder in thanks. I kissed her hand and got back to chasing the car in front of me. It was a small, two-door car, the ideal kind for travelling, since it used very little gas and was nimble enough to go around obstacles.

The car sped off, and I hadn't a hope of catching it with my big truck. I just hoped Jake's shooting had improved.

"Must be them, hang on!" I shouted. I slammed the gas pedal down, not really caring I was practically dumping gas in the street. I wanted to catch someone alive to answer some questions about these outbreaks.

"Whoa!" Jake shouted, momentarily slipping a little. He recovered quickly and aimed at the rear tires with his rifle. We were bouncing enough that I figured he wasn't going to get a shot, but Jake found a way. He just kept the gun aimed at a general point and let fly.

Fifteen shots later, the back passenger tire blew with a neat explosion, and the car careened sideways. I slowed down and parked the truck in the blind spot of the car, jumping out and grabbing my rifle. Jake ran to the side and started shooting at the windows, taking care that his shots wouldn't hit the people inside. That was a trick Julia's dad had taught us. Someone who was trying not to get shot would more likely surrender if they thought you were more than willing to ventilate their hides.

It should have worked, but it didn't. These guys had rolled out of the vehicle as neat as you could hope for, and dashed off into the homes. They paid us back for wrecking their car by firing over their shoulders, causing us to duck for cover by our vehicle. Rolling behind our truck, I didn't have a chance to shoot back, and when I did look for a shot, there was no one in sight.

"Well, shit," Jake said, changing the magazine on his rifle. "That didn't go well."

I just shook my head. "Get in the damn truck, I'm going after them." I checked to make sure a round was chambered, my knife and 'hawk were secure, and my sword was in its place on the truck. I pulled another Beretta out of the gun box on the truck, slammed a full magazine in it, and took off.

I could hear Julia call out as I ran, but there wasn't anything to say at that point. I needed to make up precious time and hoped I wouldn't get shot.

CHAPTER 17

I ran right after the pair, following the same path. The trail followed a sidewalk, and I thought I was getting close when something went "Whap!" right past my left ear. I heard the shot immediately after I ducked instinctively and kept running, hoping my next move wouldn't be met with another bullet. I saw some movement over to my right behind a small home, and I ran in that direction. Another shot sounded, but I had no idea where the bullet went.

Running through the space between two homes, I saw a pair of small-looking people climbing a fence and disappearing over the edge. They were cutting through backyards, and trying to get to the sidewalk on the other side. If I let them through, they may have enough time to ambush me when I came after them.

I cut to the right, quickly climbing a wooden fence, and bolting across the yard. I ducked under a rusty swing set, and used a small table to launch myself over the next fence. I landed heavily in the adjourning yard, just missing a trampoline. I ran around the rotted thing, and grabbed the plastic fence that closed off this yard. Swinging my legs over, I ran as fast as I could, cutting through the gate to the front yard. I figured I was one house over from where I thought they would be.

I rounded the house and pulled up short. The two were there, and one was on one knee, waiting for me to climb over the fence they just vacated. I wasn't about to walk into that trap, so I took a second to catch my breath and look over my enemy. They were small men, both wearing black clothing from head to toe. Their faces were covered with scarves, and I couldn't see any facial features. The one with the rifle kept aiming it at the fence, and I decided to make things interesting.

I took out my tomahawk and measured the distance between them and me. I was a long throw, but I had made longer ones. I took out my gun and kept it in my left hand. I didn't care of my first throw killed or maimed, I just needed them down and surprised.

A low growl came from the south and right before I cut loose, something caught their attention. Our truck came tearing around the corner, grinding the gravel and making a lot of noise. From my little corner, I could see Julia driving and Jake was shooting from the window.

The pair by the mailbox was struck stupid for a second, but it was enough to do a lot of damage. Jake managed to send enough bullets their way to hit one of them, and the other never hesitated, he just took off across the street, darting in between the houses.

I ran out to the one left behind, and even as I approached, I could see it was a waste of time. Blood poured out of a shot to the head, and this one wasn't going to tell me anything. I was mad enough to yell at Jake when Julia pulled the truck up alongside.

"Will you leave the next one to me?" I shouted, starting across the street after the second person.

"Have at it, you ungrateful prick!" Jake retorted.

"Can't get answers from a corpse, idiot!" I yelled back, running through the same two houses as the man did before me. I vaulted another fence, this one being closer to the ground and made out of metal. The wood fences were in rough shape, mostly rotten and green with algae. I had a feeling if I hit one hard enough, I'd go right through. Trouble was, I wasn't confident enough in my luck to let that experiment take place.

I saw a leg slip over the fence in front of me, so I knew I was closing in. I stretched my legs and gave it all I had, using a child's slide as a step. The fence was tall. Nevertheless, with my momentum, I grabbed the top and swung over, pulling out my tomahawk as I landed.

Across the yard, a black figure was getting close to the fence. I didn't know what he might be thinking. That fence was tall, and would have been trouble to scale in the best of circumstances.

Just as he jumped for a handhold, I let fly with my 'hawk. It embedded itself in the wood next to the man's head, causing that one to drop to the ground. He spun around, pulling two thin-bladed knives from their sheaths somewhere on his back.

I wasn't about to get into a knife fight. First of all, anyone who does will get cut, period. I don't care how good you are, you're going to get cut. Second, I leave knife fights to Jake. He seems to like them, the weirdo. Last, I have no idea if those blades have zombie goop on them, and a scratch could still kill me. I slid to a stop and pulled my pistol.

"Gunfight," I said. "Put them down." I waved the barrel of my gun at the knives which were still pointed at me.

I had to give the guy credit. He thought about it for a long moment. I could almost see the thoughts and calculations going on in his head. However, my father didn't raise a fool. I was far enough away to avoid any tricks with flipping knives at me, and I was close enough not to miss if I had to shoot.

In the seconds it took for my enemy to make up his mind, I looked over my enemy. He was about five six, with a narrow build, slender shoulders and waist. This was a really small guy, so he had to be good with those knives. He was wearing a black vest, black gloves, shirt, and pants. His face was concealed by a balaclava, and his eyes were hidden by sunglasses. In the dark, this guy would have been little more than a shadow.

"If you don't drop those knives, I'm going to start by shooting you in the knees. Then I'm aiming for your elbows. Get my drift? In one piece, or bloody and broken, doesn't matter to me," I said, taking a small step forward.

He didn't say a word; he just threw the knives to one side. Then he surprised me by reaching back and grabbing the handle of my tomahawk! He jerked forward, and stopped suddenly as the 'hawk went nowhere. I had thrown that baby pretty hard, and it wasn't going anywhere without effort.

I fired twice into the ground at his feet, kicking mud up at him. He stepped away from the tomahawk, but stopped as I fired again, keeping him from reaching the spot where his knives were.

"You're trying my patience, bub," I snarled. "I'd as soon kill you for what you've done to this community, but you're going to give up some answers first."

He said nothing; he just looked at me with those dark, sunglass eyes. I could hear the truck moving slowly down the street, passing in front of the house whose yard we were currently occupying.

"Put your hands on top of your head and turn around," I said, stepping closer. I eased the slack on the trigger of my gun, making sure it would only take a small amount of pressure to send my friend to oblivion.

He did and I moved in, first pressing the muzzle of my gun against the back of his head and grabbing the collar of his shirt. Any false move and he was going to be very dead.

CHAPTER 18

We moved to the gate, and without warning, I slammed him into it, splintering the wood around the latch and blasting our way through. His hands came off his head, but I rapped him with my gun barrel and the hands returned. This one was a thinker and given the lives he had taken without a second thought, I wasn't taking any chances.

Walking past the faded lawn ornaments, I waited until we were seen by Jake. I wasn't about to take a hand off my prisoner and flag down the truck.

"Nice work, Aaron," Jake said, coming around the truck. He kept his rifle on the man in black, so I took my hand off the man's collar, stepping to the side to be out of the line of fire in case the prisoner started something.

When I moved, I saw the man relax slightly, which told me he *was* going to try something but my moving kept it from happening. *Gonna have to watch this one*, I thought.

To save myself trouble, I ordered the man to take off his vest. "Nice and easy. Any sudden moves and I won't play nice." I was worried about another syringe or some sort of infecting device.

The man's hands didn't move. I had to admit it was a little irritating to be ignored like that. I knew he was planning something; this just seemed to be a stalling tactic. I walked around to the front of the prisoner, and without warning, I punched him in the gut. The man folded and went to one knee, gasping for air. I stepped back and looked at Jake. Something seemed wrong, though. The man wasn't making the right noises. The gasping seemed very high pitched for some reason.

Before I got too curious, Julia stepped in. "Wait a minute, Aaron." She pushed me aside, and with the tip of her spear on the man's chin, she raised his head. I could almost feel the hatred coming from behind those sunglasses, but I was stunned by what Julia said next.

"Take off the mask, bitch, or I'll open your throat." Julia shifted her stance so her hands were closer to her body. All it would take was a small thrust and several inches of sharpened steel would end all resistance.

Slowly, the hands went to the neck and pulled the balaclava and sunglasses off. Bright blue eyes stared at Julia as shoulder-length and nearly white hair tumbled out. I was surprised as hell to see I had been chasing a girl. At the same time, I felt a little guilty for punching her.

I got over it quickly enough. The girl got to her feet and spat at the two of us, much to Jake's amusement.

"Fucking heroes, huh? You're wasting your time. You're all going to die. This is just the beginning. You can't stop us all." Her words contrasted sharply with her elegant features. She had high cheekbones, which framed a pert nose, ending with a full-lipped mouth that I could see men fighting over. Julia caught me looking and gave me a stare that promised uncomfortable silence in her vicinity very soon.

Jake was staring, too, although I had a feeling he was wondering if the one he shot had been a girl, too. I gave him a chance to find out.

"Why don't you go check the other one for syringes or whatever it was they were using to infect people last night. Be careful," I said.

"Got it." Jake jumped in the truck and sped off, doubtless wanting to get to the body before someone else did, and started the whole outbreak again.

Julia smirked at the woman's predictions, but then she turned serious. "Take your vest off. My blade is still contaminated from finishing off the zombies you made. Don't make me scratch you."

That earned Julia a sneer, although I noticed the woman kept her eye on the spear as she worked to get her vest off. Once it was removed, she casually flipped it to Julia. That move was a diversion as she jumped forward, striking out with her foot and landing a blow on Julia's hip, knocking her back and causing her to lose her grip on her spear.

I whipped up my gun. "Hey! You looking to get killed?"

The prisoner laughed as Julia sprang to her feet. "Who might get hurt, pretty little bitch?" The woman taunted. "Too bad your boyfriend has a gun or I'd teach you what it means to get hurt, right before I kill you." Her beautiful features were turning very ugly as she said this.

Inwardly, I groaned. I knew Julia enough that she was not about to let this challenge pass, even though it was the smarter thing to do. Julia brushed the grass from her rear and pulled out her gun and knife. She held them out to me while never taking her eyes off her adversary.

"This may be a bad idea," I whispered, taking the weapons.

Through gritted teeth Julia hissed. "She deserves worse."

"That's my point," I said. "Don't kill her. We need what she knows." I backed away, keeping my gun pointed in the general direction of the woman in black, but away from Julia.

Our prisoner shook her pretty, evil head. "Think I'm a fool like you, stupid girl? Big boy shoots me if I win or run. No deal, although the chance to tear your pretty little face to shreds is *so* tempting." She crossed her arms and smiled, striking a taunting pose.

CHAPTER 19

Julia didn't say a word; she just walked up to the other woman and slammed a fist into her face. The prisoner's head snapped back and she fell backwards to the sidewalk. She lay there for a moment while blood streamed out of her nose. If she had been expecting Julia to bluster or talk, she found out the hard way.

Julia stepped back and shook her hand a little, waiting for the other woman to regain her feet. The white-haired girl scrambled to her feet, blood streaming from her nose. The blood had gone down the sides of her face, giving her the appearance of a deranged clown as she bared her teeth.

"I'll kill you for that, bitch." She spat blood and raised her hands, shifting forward to the attack. Her stance was classic sparring, pretty effective against untrained foes.

Julia threw a look at me. "Stay out of this one, Aaron," she said as she shook her hands and looked over her opponent.

I looked again at the other woman. She was resting lightly on her feet, with her hands slightly away from her sides. She had a sneering smile on her face, but that was the only part that was smiling. Her eyes were cold and emotionless, and I knew she would kill without hesitation. I knew also that despite Julia's admonitions to the contrary, I would step in if I had to.

"Make it quick," I said. I wanted this over with, but I also knew I couldn't stop Julia. At least, not without some serious conversations later.

"*I* will make it quick, big boy. Better say..." The woman never finished what it was I was supposed to say. Julia had leapt forward, ducked, and lashed out with her own booted foot, which slammed into the other woman's upper chest. It was a classic move used against zombies, since it knocked the dangerous ends away from you, and not into you like a kick to the stomach will. Aunt Janna perfected that one, much to Uncle Duncan's delight.

The blonde in black actually left the ground and flew backwards a bit, and landed heavily on her back. She lay there for a second, and then rose unsteadily to her feet. Her face was twisted in pain, and she looked at Julia with a mixture of hate and perhaps fear. Hatred won the coin toss and she charged forward, punching in a straight line to Julia's face.

I winced a little, as I knew what was going to happen next. I don't know who trained Blackie here, but I knew who trained Julia. Charlie James was a hard teacher, but Julia had been an apt pupil.

Blackie's punch missed as Julia shifted to the side. Julia's right hand sunk into the other woman's gut, and as she bent over, Julia's left slammed into her enemy's kidney, straightening her out again. This freed Julia's right to head north in an uppercut which cracked on Blackie's chin. That punch staggered her, giving Julia room to use a devastating punch her father had taught her. It connected right behind the other woman's ear, right where the neck and jaw connected. Done right, it stuns and hurts like hell.

Julia did it right, and Blackie crumpled to the ground. Julia bounced slightly on the balls of her feet, letting her excess energy bleed off. After a few seconds, Julia rolled the woman over onto her stomach, and secured her hands behind her back. That done, the woman was pulled to her feet.

At that moment, Jake chose to return with the truck. He hopped out and scowled when he saw our fugitive was female and bloody.

"Damn, another one," he said. "What happened to this one?"

"Uncle Charlie's neck punch," I said.

"Ouch. That explains it. Other one is dead, by the way. No syringes."

"All right. One last sweep and we'll get her to the capital," I said, relieving Julia of her prisoner. I walked her over to the truck and literally threw her into the back, stirring up a great deal of un-ladylike cursing.

"I'll ride in back," Jake said." Maybe I can get some answers." He settled himself on a wheel bump and pulled his knife.

"All right," I said as I closed the gate. "But be careful. Last time, you killed the prisoner, remember?"

"What? Oh, right. St. Charles. I remember. Okay, I'll be careful," Jake said, smiling evilly at a prisoner who looked back at him with big eyes.

I got into the truck cab with Julia, who immediately leaned in for a kiss. I obliged, naturally, and gave her a patronizing pat on the head.

"Nicely done," I said.

Julia grinned and squeezed my arm. "She wasn't even trained slightly well. Who teaches these kids these days?"

I laughed, but it got me thinking. Who did train her, and why was she so willing to kill innocents? I was pretty sure I wasn't going to like the answer, and since she was one of a pair, I wondered how many more were out there.

Great. This mess just became more complicated.

CHAPTER 20

Thankfully, the trip to the capital was boring, and Jake managed not to kill our prisoner. I took longer than I would have hoped for, but there wasn't any direct route we could take that would have made it any quicker. Clearing the secondary roads hadn't been a priority for the capital, leaving it to the communities to do as they pleased.

Julia and I didn't speak much on the way; each of us was lost in our own thoughts. I didn't know what she was thinking, but I kept returning to my father, and where he might be if he was still alive. I wanted to believe I would know it if he had died, but it had been so long I wasn't sure any more. It would be nice to get some word one way or the other.

In the back of the truck, I could see Jake talking to the prisoner, and it seemed like she was talking back. That is, she was answering his questions and not being a smart ass. It wouldn't have done her any good to try to rattle Jake. He spent so much time rattling other people he was fairly immune to it himself.

The day had turned out to be fairly bright, although it was getting colder. In a few months, it would be relatively safe to go through the city and whack a few zombies if you were so inclined. Winter was when a lot of families brought their kids to the city to see real live zombies without a great deal of danger. It was a little crazy, to be sure, but the kids needed to know what danger was out there and to be able to recognize it if there was an outbreak near where they lived. I didn't know if there was still mandatory zombie combat training in school at the capital and other communities, but it would be a shame if there weren't. Ignorance invites oblivion, as Uncle Tommy used to say.

We crossed the bridge to the capital, and I remembered from my father's journal what had happened here. I shook my head at how close the original crew had come to losing the final fight against the uprising of zombie children. Jake, Julia, and I had come close to becoming part of them, and we would have if it hadn't been for my Uncle Mike.

"Copper for your thoughts," Julia said, looking over at me.

"Just trying to work through a few memories, that's all," I said, smiling back.

"Thinking about your dad?"

"Yeah, among other things." I tried to sound nonchalant, but I don't think I convinced her.

Julia put her hand on my arm. "I miss my dad, too. I keep expecting him to suddenly appear out of the woods, tomahawks in hand, looking as dangerous as ever."

I laughed. "Not quite the image I have of *my* father, but that fits yours pretty well."

Julia laughed too, a beautiful sound in the truck cab. She turned her blue eyes on me and said seriously, "They'll come back, Aaron. When we need them the most, they'll be here."

"Do you really believe that?" I asked, not sure I believed it myself.

"It's what they do, Aaron. It's what they do."

Chapter 21

I considered that as we entered the capital. If our current situation wasn't needful enough, I hated to think how much worse things could get. We had a fringe group looking to restart the zombie apocalypse, a group of kidnappers that seemed to be shadows and smoke, and outbreaks happening all over the place and no pattern or end in sight. All we needed now was another uprising of zombie kids and we'd be three exits past Royally Screwed.

I pulled the truck into the narrow streets of the capital and made my way up the small hill towards the president's house. I felt a little weird just handing Blackie over to the authorities, but that feeling was stomped when I thought about all of the people she had infected, and all of the kids whose parents would never be coming back.

Parking the truck, I threw a wave to the President's bodyguard as I got out and received a nod in reply. Jake got out of the back and lowered the gate, and without so much as a

'Scuze me.', he dragged the woman out of the truck and dumped her on the ground. Grabbing her by the collar of her shirt, he pulled her to her feet, pushing her forward towards the fence gate. I hadn't seen Jake this upset in a while, and so I was very curious as to the extent of his conversation with Blackie in the back of the truck.

President Jackson, alerted to our presence by his guard, walked out on the porch just in time to see Jake dump the woman to the ground. I could see he was not happy with the way a prisoner was being treated, especially a woman, but he was reserving judgment by remaining quiet for the moment.

Jake walked the woman into the yard then stopped, forcing Blackie to look up at the president.

"What have you here, Jake? Why is she your prisoner?" President Jackson's voice was very precise, to the point, and slightly irritated.

"To be fair, she's your prisoner now," Jake said. "This is one of a pair of individuals who was causing the outbreak in Freeport. Her accomplice, another woman, died there. We found this." Jake held up a vial of dark fluid. "I'll give you three guesses as to what it is, but the first two don't count." Jake gave Blackie another shove, and she stumbled forward to fall at the steps of the porch.

President Jackson turned and spoke to his guard, who in turn spoke into a small radio. In five seconds, four heavily armed men raced around the house. They positioned themselves round the woman, but I noticed they kept at least two of them between the prisoner and the president. They moved very well, and seemed to be capably trained. I wouldn't look forward to a fight with any of them.

President Jackson spoke quietly, but his voice carried across the yard with ease. "Young lady, you are in a lot of trouble. For your recent activities, you could be executed immediately, and I doubt anyone here would mourn your passing. But I would see a cessation of these outbreaks, and you are going to give us as much information as you have. You will decide how that interrogation will go, but I caution you against any bravado. It will not serve you in any way."

Blackie sneered and then spit on the lawn. For half a second, I thought President Jackson's guard was going to shoot her on the spot. His face flashed in rage for a split second before he recovered.

"Your arrogance is duly noted. However, it will not help you any further. Robert," President Jackson spoke to the man behind him. "Take this person to the detention center, and place her in the lower level. She is to be secured, and then searched. I want Brenda on this; she will know what to do and what to look for."

Robert snapped a quick salute then went inside for a second. Coming back outside, he was carrying a small duffle bag, which he placed in front of Blackie. He took out handcuffs and leg irons, and when the prisoner was secured to his satisfaction, he placed a small black hood over her head. When finished, he took Blackie by the arm and walked her out of the yard and down the street. He was followed by three of the guards. The fourth went onto the porch and took the position normally reserved for Robert.

President Jackson turned to us and waved us inside. Once seated around a table, he spoke directly. "Thanks for your help. Were you able to get any information on your trip back here that might be of any help?" He spoke to all of us, but the question was directed to Jake.

"I didn't bother with the why of the situation, since it really wasn't important and a waste of time to bother asking," Jake said. The president seemed to mull that one over for a second before nodding slightly.

"I did find out that they were planning something bigger, once I figured out how to read between the insults, threats to my sacred well-being, and the destruction of all I held dear. When I tried to find out what it was, she changed tactics and tried to get me mad enough to kill her. I could have, easily, especially when she told me she enjoyed infecting children the most, but by then I knew she was just trying to cause an incident," Jake continued. "When I questioned her about where she was from, I got a curious answer."

"What was that?" President Jackson asked.

I was curious too, and leaned in like the rest of the listeners.

"She said nowhere that I would ever dare to go, being a 'chicken shit towner' as she called me, "Jake said. "I don't think she meant to say that last out loud, but I think it's important."

President Jackson leaned back and looked at the ceiling. "I wonder what she meant. If she thought you were a 'towner', which I can only assume meant you were a person who lived in an established community, then she must live in either a remote area outside the communities, like you do, or someplace else, although I can't think of where that might be."

Julia spoke up. "She had to learn her hatred of communities. She's too young to have formed that opinion on her own. She also has no fear of hurting kids. That's not something you see in any community.

I nodded. "It makes sense. It also suggests someone has been holding a grudge against society for a long time, and decided the time was right to strike out."

Jake shook his head. "Why now? What's different about now, as opposed to say five or ten years later, or even a few years earlier? I don't understand the timing."

President Jackson stood up, signaling the meeting was over. "I think we will find out those answers in due time. In the meanwhile, you might want to take that vial over to the medical center. I imagine you'd prefer not to have it break open in your pocket."

CHAPTER 21

Jake nodded and Julia and I made sure there was plenty of space between Jake and us as we left the presidential home and headed up the street to the medical center. There were a lot of people about, and a few looked at us curiously. Several were not shy about pointing at us as we walked up the road, and I could see Jake was slightly irritated by the tightening of his jaw and the narrowing of his eyes.

"What's everyone's deal?" Jake asked of no one in particular. "Why are we so popular?"

I couldn't let that one go even if I had tried. "Maybe it's because we're so darned good looking."

Jake snorted. "I'll buy that for Julia, but you're a sight. You got your ass kicked by an ugly tree."

I casually punched Jake in the arm, causing him to stumble to the side. He swung back, but there wasn't any effort in it, since he missed by a mile. We walked up to the medical building and found it was closed for the day. I thought that was weird at first, but I guess that people had to go home sometime. It was getting later in the evening, so we would have to decide if we were going to stay here of head back home. I put the question to Jake and Julia.

Jake groaned. "I'd rather head home, we could be there before it was too dark. Besides, we don't have a great track record when it comes to this place."

I couldn't argue with that, since Jake had killed a man here and I had fought with several myself. But all arguments flew out the window when Julia spoke up.

"Let's stay! We need to get cleaned up anyway, and we could go to dinner and stay in one of the inns like normal people. Please please please please please pleeeese?" Julia looked up at me with big eyes and blinked rapidly. On her beautiful face, it just looked ridiculous. I couldn't do anything but laugh.

Jake grunted. "Well, there goes my plan. All right, where do you want to stay? By the way, I still have zombie virus in my pocket."

I wrapped Julia up in a hug and walked back the way we came. "Let's get back to the truck and park it somewhere closer to an inn. We'll secure the virus at the truck; I think there's a container there. We'll find a place to stay, clean up, and go eat. Objections?"

Julia wrapped her arms around my neck and did a pull up to kiss me. I took that as a no. Jake just shook his head. I didn't think I'd get a kiss from him.

We drove the truck to the edge of town and secured our cargo with one of the storage managers. He put everything into a small shed and locked it, handing us the key. If anything happened to our stuff while he was on watch, he'd catch hell and he knew it. This was his business and he took it seriously. As far as I knew, no one had ever stolen anything from under his careful eye.

Walking down the main street, we took in the general feel of the place. People were bustling about, a few stopped to wave and say hi. However, there was still a kind of pall over the area, like something was out of kilter. As I walked, I watched people storing wood and topping off water supplies for winter. We were about two months away from not having much in the way of rain and the river sometimes froze over.

We decided to splurge and spend our night at the most luxurious hotel in the capital. It was a four story stone building that looked out over the river. We could have parked our truck in the parking garage that made up the interior of the building, but we would have had to carry all of our stuff into our rooms.

At the front desk, I signed us in for three rooms, and Jake snorted again, but he got over it quickly when Julia stared at him hard enough to draw blood. I opted for the river view rooms with the balconies, and paid the outrageous sum of two silver pieces per room. It was a lot, and could have bought a decent amount of supplies, but since we were extremely well off in terms of money, I didn't mind a little splurge. That was a benefit of being a former collector. I could go anywhere and get what I wanted without too much fuss.

We went into our separate rooms and I quickly took off my weapons and dirty clothes. I was somewhat amused to see how much weaponry I actually carried on myself when I went zombie hunting. Two knives, a tomahawk, a pistol, three loaded magazines, and a sword. I was surprised my back didn't hurt from all that hardware.

After my shower, which was nicely warm, I put on my spare pants and stood out on the balcony drying myself with the evening breeze. It was cool but I kind of liked it. With my shirt off, I felt like some kind of ancient warrior immune to the elements. The first stiff wind would likely send me scurrying for cover, but I indulged my fantasy for a second.

Figuring I had a moment before everyone was ready, I got out my kerosene spray and brought my blades out to the small table on the balcony. I sprayed my knives first, burning off any virus that may be sticking around. I didn't see any red flames, so that was a good sign. I wasn't going to have to make another sheath this time. My 'hawk burned red for a while, but since I used it the most, that wasn't a surprise. My sword took the longest, because it was so big, but it was always fun to hold that flaming sword up like a torch. One of these days, I was going to burn myself being silly, but not today. When the flames died, I realized it was a good thing I was on the top floor or I might have scared the hell out of anyone above me.

After the burning, I pulled out a piece of steel wool and a small bottle of oil. Fine steel wool was useful stuff. It could clean a weapon, polish some metal, and small bits could start a fire. I rubbed each blade until they were shiny, then worked a bit of oil around to keep things from rusting. My weapons were all carbon steel, and they needed care. My sword made me grateful it was cool out, as I really had to work that big boy.

When I was done, I looked up and was surprised to see Julia looking at me from her own balcony. She was wearing just a towel, and her wet blonde hair was pulled back behind her ears. She looked absolutely stunning, and I felt something turn over in my chest as I smiled at her.

"How was your shower?" I asked, putting my blades away.

"Warm. Lovely." Julia looked at me through lowered lashed. "Lonely," she added.

I went over to the railing that separated us, reached over and pulled her close for a lone kiss. "Behave yourself," I said, with not a small amount of regret.

Julia grinned wickedly at me. "If you say so." She turned away and in the same motion, dropped her towel as she went back into her room. I had a glimpse of slender, athletic legs rising up to perfectly rounded buttocks. I tried to see more, but she closed the bedroom door and I had to keep from falling over the railing.

Behind me, a voice sniggered. "Jackass."

CHAPTER 22

I spun around and saw Jake standing there. He was holding a burning knife and grinning at me with the most annoying look that he could put on his face, which was impressive.

I decided not to rise to the occasion, metaphorically speaking, since physically I was already halfway there. "Your time will come," I croaked, having had my mouth go suddenly dry a few seconds ago.

Jake cocked his head as he studied his burning knife. "That a threat? Not like you, Aaron."

I shook my head. "No, stupid. Someday you'll fall in love, too."

Jake's smile turned real. "You feel that strong, huh? Good for you. Everybody should at some point." His voice turned more serious. "Hope she feels the same way, bro."

I hadn't thought about it, and suddenly I was scared. I mean, I knew she cared about me, but what if she didn't feel the same way? What if I told her and made a complete fool out of myself? I couldn't possibly live in the same place as she, knowing she didn't feel like I did. I decided not to say anything until she did. That way I would know for sure, and then not feel stupid.

"Well, I'll let her tell me first, then I'll know," I said, gathering up my blades and 'hawk.

"Good plan," Jake said.

I couldn't tell if he was being supportive or sarcastic, and right then I really didn't care.

We all got ourselves together enough to go and get something to eat. We were dressed casual, but each of us had a weapon on us somewhere. It was too much of a habit not to. Julia was all flirty smiles and I felt like my heart was going to burst, but I tried to play it cool. Jake saw my dilemma and was openly grinning at me like the jerk he was.

At the restaurant, was sat near a table at the back, and the place was reasonably full, which was good for the business, and for things in general. A lot of the patrons were old timers, reliving the good old days. If a meal out was becoming the norm for a lot of people, then things may finally be returning to what my dad had talked about before the Upheaval. It was something to think about.

Halfway into our meal, a gorgeous blonde walked into the restaurant. She was wearing tight jeans and a form-fitting shirt that left nothing to the imagination. Her knee-high boots were shiny black, and she wore a vest which accented her ample charms. Her long hair hung in a way that framed her face, and her eyes were taunting and contemptuous at the same time. She was a woman to fight for, and many had, if I recalled correctly. All conversation seemed to stop when she looked around. Spotting our table, she strutted across the room, clearly aware of the effect she was having. Julia did the same thing, only she wasn't aware of her effects.

"Hey beautiful," the blonde said, sitting next to Julia and giving her a kiss on the cheek.

Julia gave her a hug. "Hey yourself, Kayla. I didn't know you were going to stay in the capital."

"I'm over at the Towers. Took a room by the river." Kayla leaned behind Julia and gave me a hug. "Hey, Aaron. Looking as deadly as ever."

"Thanks, Kayla. How's your mom?" I asked, taking a drink of wine.

"Better, thanks. Dad was worried for a while, but she's her old self. Wants her niece and nephews to visit more often. Hey, gorgeous." Kayla directed that last at Jake, who smiled.

"Hey yourself," Jake said as he reached out and gave Kayla's hand a squeeze, causing her to blush slightly.

"Thanks for your help, lately, I really appreciate it," I said, working around another mouthful of food.

Kayla smiled and put her elbows on the table, resting her head on folded hands. "Well, let's talk about that, Aaron. I was wondering if I could tag along and help on a more permanent basis."

I thought about it, but before I could say anything, Julia spoke up.

"Are you sure, Kay? I mean, you've been as trained as we have, but we've logged a lot more experience being collectors and all. It's a dangerous thing and there's not much gold at the end of that rainbow, if you get my meaning." Julia sounded sincere, and I was grateful she was able to voice what I been thinking.

"Serious as a heart attack, baby. I want to be part of the action. I mean, I grew up on the stories of our parents, yours especially, and now you're out there making the same kind of history. I want to be part of it, and in a way, I ought to be." Kayla smiled and I had to admit she did have a point. As the daughter of Duncan and Janna Fries, she'd know a thing or two about defending herself.

I looked over at Jake. "What say thee, oh eldest brother?"

Jake shrugged. "As long as you understand you could be killed at any time, and your death will likely be messy, I'm okay with it." Jake softened his words a bit. "I think you'd be a good addition, personally."

Julia tossed a breadstick at Jake, and then turned to Kayla. "Cool. Then if you don't mind, maybe we can do some training together. I've only had these lunks to fight with."

Kayla beamed while Jake and I exchanged hurt looks.

"What next?" I asked.

Jake looked at the door. "I think 'What Next?' just walked in."

CHAPTER 23

I looked over to the door and saw what Jake was looking at. The sheriff was standing there, and he was clearly uncomfortable with the thought of disturbing people while they ate. However, he overcame it quickly enough when he saw us in the corner and came to join us.

"Gentlemen, ladies. May I have a word with you?" the sheriff asked.

Jake pulled a chair from a nearby empty table. "Have a seat, sheriff. Can we get you something to eat?"

Sheriff Tucker shook his head. "No, I won't bother you for that long. I wanted to make you aware of a situation we have here and to maybe ask you for help."

Intrigued, I leaned forward. "Do tell. Might this have anything to do with the kidnappings we have heard so much about?"

Tucker shook his head. "I'm at my wits end. We've had stakeouts, and we've had citizen patrols. Hell, I even thought of having papers made for everybody and if you didn't have one you were a suspect." Lane shook his head. "Of course, I brought that one to the president and his guard nearly shot me. Those old timers take their rights pretty seriously."

"For some of them, their rights and their lives were all they had left after the Upheaval," Jake said quietly.

Tucker looked at Jake sideways before continuing. "Anyway, my men are all known around here, and this group is operating outside my range of experience. They used to take one every few months, and sometimes we would find out it was a girl running off with her boyfriend. Now, it's getting so they're not just taking the young girls, but the older ones, too. Hell, last month we lost a mother of three for God's sake!"

Julia put her hand to her mouth and Kayla seemed distraught as well. Jake's eyes narrowed and I could feel my own anger start at a low simmer. We might have run into them a while back, but being the young, misguided, and idealistic fools we were, we let them and their boss live.

"What do you want us to do?" I asked, giving voice to the question that I knew was on everyone's mind.

"I don't know!" Tucker's voice raised a little and a few people looked our way. He glanced around and lowered his volume. "I don't know. I feel so damn helpless, and I know there's going to be another kidnapping soon. I can feel it."

Jake spoke up. "Tell you what, sheriff. You've told us you have a problem you can't solve. All right, done on your part. We'll see what we can do and let you know how it goes. If we can catch one of them, we'll see what he has to say. Just do me the favor of telling your boys we're out there so they don't come after us by mistake."

"Done. And you're doing more than I could ask for. Thanks, I really appreciate it." Sheriff Tucker's gratitude was real and he left walking a little straighter than when he came in.

Jake turned to the rest of us. "Any ideas?"

"Nope," I said.

"None," said Julia.

"Zip," said Kayla. "But..."

Jake cocked his head her way. "But...what? Talk to me and let's see if you're as suspicious as I am."

Kayla kissed her lips at Jake. "You know me, sweetness. What are the odds the sheriff happens to have a problem with kidnappings getting worse just as we are in town? What are the odds that he has a feeling the same night we decide to stay the night?"

I would be the first to admit I am too trusting and would likely have never thought there was a connection. However, now that Kayla had brought it up, there *were* a lot of coincidental events happening.

Jake signaled the waiter. "We'll have to see what happens. If it turns out Tucker is on the level, then we're all good. If not, then we need to expect an ambush." Jake looked over at Kayla. "Sure you still want part of this?"

Kayla gave my brother a smile that was a lot of unfulfilled promises. It made me sweat and I wasn't even the recipient. Jake wasn't fazed at all, the cold jerk.

"As much as I can get, gorgeous," she said.

CHAPTER 24

Half an hour later, and another bottle of wine found us with a flawed but workable plan. One of us would act as bait and the others would follow, surprising the kidnappers if they decided to make a move. The upside of the plan would be the kidnappers would be biting off a whole lot of trouble from either of the two lovely ladies. The downside was we could lose one of the two lovely ladies.

An hour later, I was in a yard standing next to a small tree, hoping like hell the owners of the house wouldn't see me and decide to say howdy by shooting me in the ass. It wasn't a situation I would have recommended to anyone, but since it was the best idea out of the several we had thought of, it would have to do.

When we left the restaurant, we had agreed to split up, and we would position ourselves along a predetermined route for our victim to walk down. Once she passed one of us, we would run up a parallel street and reposition, leapfrogging the other saviors. The theory was we would be in place before the attack came, able to intervene as needed. It wasn't a great plan, but we couldn't hunt like we normally would, and since we weren't sure what we were looking for anyway, it would serve.

The night was cool and getting colder, and I wished I had a heavier shirt on. The house behind me was dark, and I was grateful they couldn't see me, if they were still awake. I looked down the street, hoping to catch a glimpse of Jake or Julia, but I knew I wouldn't. Jake wouldn't answer if I called to him, and that would defeat the whole purpose of being stealthy.

The sky was overcast, and the darkness was deep. I could barely make out much detail even thought my eyes were adjusted to the dark. Some of the shadows were as black as the bottom of a well. Nevertheless, it was very quiet, and I was able to make sounds out around me. There was a cat across the street that was talking to itself, chirping and meowing. I heard some movement in the house behind me, and when I focused on it, I realized why the people living there weren't looking out their windows. The rhythmic creaking going on up on the second floor told me exactly what *they* were doing.

I tried to ignore that noise and focus on the drunken singing that was coming down the street. On the far sidewalk, a woman was singing softly to herself, weaving slightly from side to side. She bumped into a small tree, burped, and giggled like a little girl as she spun nearly completely around. Catching herself, she scolded the tree and slapped it with her hand before she continued on her way. Even in the darkness, I could tell she was an attractive blonde, a perfect target for anyone looking to do a nefarious deed, kidnapping or otherwise.

Kayla kept up her act as I watched her go by. It was a decent distraction from the house behind me, since the couple had started talking strangely to each other. It was some of the stupidest crap I had ever heard. Why the man would be interested in whom his wife's daddy was at that particular moment made no sense at all.

I was paying attention to the wrong thing and nearly missed the dark figure which flitted up the street behind Kayla. It was a tall man, too tall to be Jake and clearly not able to be Julia. He moved from deep shadow to deep shadow, trying to stay out of the lighter areas in case his victim turned around suddenly. As I watched him move, I realized he could potentially use my hiding place as a stopping point. That would be interesting. I knew Jake and Julia were further down the street, so I would have to deal with this. If I could, I'd try to take the man alive and hand him over to the sheriff. If not, I wasn't going to cry about it.

The man passed my spot, and as he moved, so did I. I quietly drew my grandfather's knife from its sheath, and if I didn't know better, I'd swear it gave a little quiver of anticipation. The man following Kayla was so focused on his target that he didn't notice me step in behind him. A good rule to follow: In the dark, move when your prey moves. They can't see your movement unless you're right in front of them.

Despite my bulk, I had learned to be stealthy from the master, and this guy wasn't about to notice me.

I stopped in a deep shadow, since I realized that the man hadn't done anything yet. If I had attacked him, it would be my fault and he could claim he was just going home.

As it turned out, I did the right thing. A second man was coming up the street, as quietly as the first, only this one was on the far side of the road. Had I kept walking, I would have blown the whole thing.

I watched the second man move quickly to catch up, and Kayla was still moving down the street, as oblivious as ever. She stumbled a bit, caught herself on a fence, and had a hushed conversation with her fingernails, which caused her to giggle again.

As the second man passed me, the first one had closed the distance with Kayla. He stepped up behind her and grabbed her around the waist and shoulders. Her arms were pinned to her sides and his hand was clamped over her mouth. He lifted her off her feet to disorient her, and when she kicked out with her feet, the second man arrived. He caught up her kicking legs and wrapped them up in his arms. The two men began to run side by side down the street, holding a squirming Kayla between them. The whole attack had taken barely seconds.

I broke into a sprint, while at the same time, I realized I had no plan of attack that wasn't a risk to Kayla. I didn't have a gun with me, although a shot was out of the question. I had my knife, and I had my fists. Hopefully, they would be enough. As I ran, I wondered where the Julia and Jake were. I had seen no sign of them and hoped they were close.

CHAPTER 25

The two men ahead of me slowed to a stop, and their manner of stopping told me they had just encountered something and were contemplating their next move. A man stood in the middle of the street, and it was clear by his stance he had been expecting them. His hands were behind his waist, seemingly clasped. His face was concealed by shadow, but I didn't need light to know who it was.

As the men stopped about fifteen yards from him, Jake pulled his hands out from behind his back, each holding a long, gently curved knife in each hand. The blades were seven inches long, and even in the darkness they gleamed with malicious intent. Jake leapt forward, not bothering to waste time talking or boasting. He never bothered anyway.

The man holding Kayla's legs dropped them and jumped towards Jake, pulling a knife out from a sheath on his thigh. He moved forward in a low crouch, holding his knife low and to the side, likely hoping for a chance to slide the point in between Jake's ribs.

I didn't have a chance to watch Jake's fight, as I was closing on the man still holding Kayla. However, this time surprise wasn't on his side and she knew what he intended to do. He tried to hold her feet off the ground, but that was precisely what she wanted him to do. She kicked her feet out to give them momentum as she thrust her boot heels back into the man's knees.

I heard a stifled cry as the man fell forward. I had no way to stop them, but I shouldn't have worried. Kayla twisted as they went down and managed to get the man underneath her as they hit the ground. She jerked her head back, slamming the back part into the man's face, eliciting another cry. That also freed her from one of his arms, and she used that opportunity to slam her elbow into the man. Rolling off, Kayla came up with one knee on the man's chest.

The man was game, however. He got his hands under the knee on his chest and thrust backwards, spilling Kayla off of him. As she fell, he scrambled to his feet, pulling his own knife. Just as he advanced, I slammed into him from behind. I had a full head of steam and my shoulder was down, with my hand tucked into a fist on my chest. His arms and legs flew outwards and his neck snapped back as I hit him. I straightened my back as I hit him, causing the man to swap ends and land on his face. Somewhere between earth and sky, he had lost his knife, but I wasn't worried about that anymore.

Kayla jumped to her feet and lightly punched me on the arm. "That was awesome! I think he flew ten feet!" She whispered excitedly.

I ignored her as I went to see if Jake needed any help. The guy I hit wasn't going anywhere. I heard soft footfalls behind me and was relieved to see Julia coming up the street.

Jake and the other man were squared off, each looking for an opening to thrust or cut. Jake held his left hand knife in a reverse grip, while his right one was held in a normal fashion. I was surprised and impressed with the fact the man was still standing. He must have had some skill for Jake to have left him alive this long.

Julia came up to Kayla to make sure she was okay. I started to circle the combatants when Jake glanced my way and shook his head slightly. I knew when to back off, so I started to go over to the man I had downed to see if he was in any shape to answer questions.

I never got the chance. Julia suddenly hissed and pulled her weapons, and Kayla armed herself as well. Out of the side streets, six more men advanced on us, and the hatchets and knives they carried weren't there for show. I pulled my second knife and watched as two men came at me.

"Jake! Finish it and get over here," I said in a loud whisper.

Jake's answer was just a low growl, which was enough. He had seen the activity and didn't like it at all. I didn't like the fact that Jake had been right about Tucker.

Julia and Kayla stood close together, facing opposite directions. Julia had a long thin needle of a blade which cut quicker than sarcasm, and she had wrapped her belt around her other hand, leaving about a foot dangling with her heavy buckle at the end. It was crude but effective at either smacking the shit out of someone or trapping someone else's weapon.

I didn't waste time. I ducked low, knocked aside a thrust, and jammed my grandfather's knife to the hilt into the closest man's solar plexus. I twisted the blade and yanked it out, throwing a rope of blood into the street. I pushed the falling man into the path of the second man, and lashed out with my foot as he stepped aside. I connected with his knee and put him down on all fours with a startled gasp. He stuck his knife up in defense and I caught a piece of it on my sleeve as I thrust with my other knife, jamming it into his eye socket. The knife stuck and I let go as he fell, turning to the other men. I managed to see Jake head butt his opponent, and then use the opening to jam both knives onto the man's throat. He went down to his knees, grasping his throat and dying in a moist, noisy manner.

The man I had initially hit was no longer with us, as He made the mistake of trying to get up and Kayla stabbed him in the back of the neck. There was a small pause as the remaining men sized up their position. Jake pulled his knives out of the dead man and wiped them off, never taking his eyes off the enemy. He then whipped his hand out and impaled another man in the upper chest, right where the neck met the torso. The man fell to the ground, looking down at the knife handle which suddenly had sprouted from his sacred person. He raised a weak hand to try and pull it out, but he fell over and died as his lungs filled with blood, his feet drumming a fading beat on the road.

The last three suddenly found themselves outnumbered, but they were motivated by something, since they didn't take the chance to run and instead moved to attack. One of them charged towards Julia, and she wiped him out by first popping him in the face with her buckle, then slitting his throat as neat as you please. Blood sprayed out, looking black in the darkness.

Jake finished the fifth man almost casually, blocking a clumsy slice and punching his other knife into the man's chest about five times before letting him drop.

The last man was big, probably the leader, as this group was likely ruled by the strongest. His long curved knife was more like a short sword, and it gave him the advantage of reach. He muttered something inarticulate and slashed at me, missing as I ducked. I cut at his leg and danced back to avoid a backswing that would have taken my head off.

He followed that swing with a quick overhand cut, much faster than I thought him capable of. Turns out, he was big and fast. I batted the incoming bade away and stepped in closer, removing his advantage of reach. I stabbed him in the upper arm, piercing his bicep to the bone. He dropped the knife and gripped his arm, cursing me as he stepped back. I didn't want to give him the chance to run, so I slammed the steel pommel of the knife onto his forehead, stunning him momentarily. I followed that with a punch to his chin, dropping him for good and putting him out of the fight.

CHAPTER 26

Behind me, Jake and the girls were cleaning up, wiping off their weapons and moving the bodies off the street. The neighborhood was going to awaken with a hell of a surprise in the morning. I guarded the lone survivor, standing behind him as he sat and holding the point of his little sword at the base of his neck. Any sudden moves would kill him, and he knew it.

Jake searched the bodies and assembled a small pile of weapons and coins. There was a motley assortment of knives and guns, and Jake showed me sixteen newly minted, heavy silver coins. It was a tidy sum for murder. These men had been paid to kill us, and the question remained as to who and how.

I spoke quietly to the back of the man's head. "Who sent you after us?"

The man spoke sullenly. "Don't know what you're talking about. We were drinking with friends, and on the way home, we got separated. We caught up to our buddies just as you were attacking them and tried to come and help them." He didn't try to pull away from the knife at his neck.

I looked at Jake who shook his head. The story actually sounded plausible, but there was a flaw in it, too. "If you were so worried about your friends, why not use your guns? Between the eight of you, I counted four guns."

"Take a shot in this neighborhood and the law is on you in no time," the man said. He looked up at me. "You're gonna hang for murder, you know that? I'm gonna enjoy watching you swing." The man spat and gripped his injured arm tighter.

Julia and Kayla exchanged a look, and for a second, even I felt it could be seen that way, especially when no one else saw the two dead men pick up Kayla. But Jake squatted down in front of the man and looked into his eyes.

"You're a liar, and would you like to know why?" Jake asked.

"Fuck you, murderer, I ain't talking," the man said, staring right back.

Jake continued. "All of you are wearing shit clothes and run-down shoes. Your weapons are filthy and your guns probably wouldn't fire if you tried them. Three of them don't even have bullets. Yet, all of you are carrying brand new silver. No other money, just these coins, and in the exact same amount. Coincidence?"

The man looked away, then looked back as Jake continued.

"We had no business to walk these streets, we were just having dinner. Yet all of a sudden we are here and you assholes are sharing the same space with nefarious intent. Coincidence?" Jake asked again.

The man gave no answer, but he was starting to show signs of agitation. Jake looked down on the man.

"How is it that the sheriff can afford to pay you like that?" Jake inquired.

"It ain't his. He just..." The man stopped himself, and then cursed as he realized he had said too much.

Jake smiled in the dark. "Thank you for your cooperation. I will assume then that Tucker isn't the mastermind behind the kidnappings, but rather the middle man between the ones wanting the girls and the ones getting the girls." Jake grabbed the man and pulled him to his feet. "If you shout, I gut you. If you run, I'll cut your tendons and drag you. If you try to fight, I'll cut your eyes out. Understand?"

The defeated man nodded and I gave the long knife to Kayla, who put it with the bundle of weapons she was carrying. We walked silently down the streets, heading back towards the river area. Our destination was the president's house, since it would have been stupid to go to the sheriff.

At the president's house, silent men were keeping watch in the darkness. One of them detached himself from a shadow and came out to meet us.

"House is closed, no visitors until morning," he said, adjusting the heavy automatic weapon slung around his shoulder.

"Not visiting, just dropping off," Jake said. "This man is part of the kidnapping going on around here. Seven more of his friends are lying on the street eight blocks north of here."

The guard looked surprised. "I'll be damned. Well, why bring him here? Take him over to Sheriff Tucker."

Jake shook his head. "Tucker's the contact here for the operation. These men were sent to ambush us as we were trying to ambush them. Tucker set us up for that."

The guard nodded and swung his weapon around. He spoke quietly into his radio and another man joined us in the darkness by the presidential gate. This guy was huge, at least two inches taller than my better and me by about twenty pounds; none of it fat. His face looked like it was carved from granite, inflexible and unmovable. He probably ate steel washers for breakfast. His trained eyes quickly scanned the situation and us, lingering a little on Jake and me.

"Lem, these kind folks have brought us a gift. The man they have here tried, with his friends, to ambush and murder these youngsters," the first guard said. "They were trying to stop the kidnapping going on around here."

Lem grunted a deep, ominous sound from his large chest. "Really." He leaned over and grasped the prisoner by the collar of his shirt. "My little sister was kidnapped last year. You and I are going to have a deep, meaningful conversation." Lem dragged the now whimpering man away.

The first guard watched them go, and then turned back to us. "I'll send men to clean up the bodies. In the morning, we'll collect the sheriff. Come back around ten, if you can."

I nodded and we walked away, eager to go back to our hotel and comfortable beds. Julia walked beside me, wrapping an arm around my waist. Kayla and Jake were talking in low tones behind us, but I didn't feel like talking myself. I just wanted this day and night to be over with and wanted to go to sleep. The wine had given me a sight headache and I just wanted to rest. Julia seemed to understand and she stayed quiet, looking up at me occasionally to smile.

All in all, it had been a good day.

CHAPTER 27

"You've got to be kidding me."

"Nope. That's the way it went down, and that's what he said. Why would he lie at that point?"

President Jackson shook his head. He looked tired, more tired than perhaps he should, bet then there were a lot of thing going on in his world that didn't make sense. This was another layer of stress. I felt somewhat bad for the man, but I reminded myself he chose to run for office, and I was just a spectator to the conversation anyway.

Jake continued. "If your men cleaned up the mess from last night, and they said they would, then Tucker might not yet know everything was a failure and we have a prisoner. As far as we know, there weren't any witnesses."

The president sighed. "I'm starting to envy your father. When he was president, all he had to worry about were hordes of zombies killing everyone. This peacetime administering really makes me long for the good old days when I knew who my enemies were." He signaled his guard, Robert. "Take two men and pick up Tucker. If he has any deputies around, bring them in, too. I want this kept quiet. If word gets out that the sheriff had a hand in the kidnappings, there's going to be trouble."

Robert nodded and left. Jackson turned back to us. "Got another bit of fun for you. Message came in this morning. Feel like another run at your luck?"

Outwardly, I was calm, but inside I was vigorously shaking my head. Last night was a blur, and when we got back to the hotel, I wanted another shower. Julia joined me this time and it was the most amazing shower of my life. We made love in the cascading water and continued our new adventures in the bedroom. If I thought I was in love before, last night stamped it fully on my soul. I think I finally understand what my mom meant to my dad, and I don't know what I would do if Julia were to be taken from me.

Of course, Jake knew immediately what had happened, and arched a single eyebrow at me as acknowledgement. Kayla and Julia had their heads together the entire time we had walked over to the president's house. I would have loved to know what they were talking about, and yet at the same time, I know I preferred not to.

Now we were throwing ourselves back into the mix. All I wanted to do was go home and just live quietly for a while. However, that seemed like a far away dream as Jake and the president kept talking.

"What's the mess this time?" Jake was asking.

In answer, President Jackson pulled out a faded road map that had a lot of intersecting lines across it. Out of habit, I quickly referenced our current position and the location of our home.

"We've received reports from three different communities along the grey corridor talking about increased zombie activity. There's always been some there, as you know, but there has been a large uptick and it's too coincidental to think it's random," Jackson said, pointing to three towns along the stretch of old I-57. They weren't directly on the interstate. Those towns had been wiped out early during the Upheaval when people were running from the apocalypse, even though it was waiting for them wherever they were going.

"What kind of activity? How much?" Jake asked, running a finger down the highway on the map.

"I don't think it's what you guys have been dealing with lately. I think word has finally gotten around and people are taking extra precautions and are much more wary of strangers. Freeport was, I think and hope, the last we'll see of that kind of thing. No, this seems to be more of an old threat coming back to become a new one." President Jackson sighed as he looked at the map. "What next?"

I spoke up at that rhetorical question. "I've learned it's best not to ask. That's when fate pays attention and gets her black sense of humor on."

"Or lack thereof. If I can persuade you to tackle this task, then I think we can rest for a small time," the president said.

"No, actually we can't," Jake said.

"No?"

"No. We still don't know who is responsible for the attacks and the attempts to re-create the Upheaval. I've got another vial of zombie crap in storage, and the kidnappings have been halted for the time being, but someone was behind those, too. I'd bet my last gold piece that Tucker wasn't the end of the line. In fact, he couldn't be. Where would he stash the girls and for what purpose? Nowhere around here," Jake said.

President Jackson narrowed his eyes and looked at Jake more closely. Then he smiled slightly, putting a hand on Jake's shoulder.

"You're much more like your father than you may think or want to admit. He had the ability to look at the big picture better than most people," he said.

Jake shook his head. "Well, if he bothers to show up, send him south. I could use the help. Good day."

CHAPTER 28

Jake left the room and I nodded my goodbye to the president. Julia and Kayla followed us and we walked steadily out of the area, heading up towards our truck. By the set of his shoulders, I knew Jake wasn't interested in talking right now, so I decided to just walk and take a look around as the town went about its daily morning activities. There weren't too many people about, and I doubted the word about Tucker had gotten very far, if at all. If the president's guards were worth their weight, then the most anyone would know about the truth would be rumors.

When we reached a junction that took us to the medical center in one direction and the truck in another, I stopped and waited for Jake to figure out I wasn't following him. Julia and Kayla stopped as well, and the three of us looked at Jake as he looked quizzically at us.

"Aren't you coming to the truck?" He asked.

"Are we coming back here?" I responded.

"Yeah, so?"

I smiled. Doesn't take four of us to carry a vial. We'll wait here. Don't worry. We'll talk about you."

Jake shook his head and muttered something about lazy jerks as he turned and walked off.

While we waited, Julia took the opportunity to jump into my arms, wrap her legs around me, and kiss me deeply. I returned the kiss equally, taking in her essence and falling for her all over again. Kayla grinned in the morning sun and chided us both.

"Get back to your rooms, you two, geez," she said.

I put Julia down with another kiss. "If we did that, you'd be out here by yourself with Jake. Not sure Julia's ready for that," I replied.

Julia ran a hand around my belt line. "I could handle it," she said, with a little gleam I her eye.

I laughed, happy to be alive this morning and have this girl on my side. "No doubt. But I'm not sure I could."

Julia let me go and stood in front of me, looking up at me with big serious eyes. "There is still unfinished business, mister."

"Like what?" I asked, slightly perplexed.

"Anything you want to tell me?"

I thought for a minute, recalling the conversation I had with Jake the night before. "No, not really. You pretty much know all the stories behind my scars now," I said with a grin. In a lower voice, I added, "Not in front of Kayla, anyway."

Julia harrumphed and turned to Kayla, who just smiled and shrugged. I knew I was getting into unfamiliar territory at lightning speed, and hoped like crazy Jake was going to get back soon. Give me a zombie to kill or a man to fight any day. This emotional sparring with females was way beyond me.

Fortunately, Jake appeared before things got worse, so we headed back over to the health center. Jake led the way, with Kayla by his side. Julia was with me, and we hung back a bit, watching the two of them.

"Think they'll ever wind up like us?" I asked, nodding towards the couple ahead.

Julia shrugged. "Maybe. Kayla would love it, but I'm not sure Jake is willing to settle down."

"Kayla wants to be with Jake?" I asked, startled. This was news to me. I figured she could have her pick of men, and Jake wasn't the best of company. I said so to Julia.

"Why not Jake?" Julia answered. "He's well trained, lives in a grand hotel on a huge estate, is independently wealthy, and the son of one of the most famous men in the country. Not to mention he's pretty good-looking as well," Julia observed.

I thought about that and soothed my ego. "I'm taller."

Julia laughed out loud, causing Kayla and Jake to turn around. She covered her mouth with her hand and I just grinned and shrugged as if she was crazy. Jake scowled, but Kayla turned him back to the task at hand.

We entered the health facility and the receptionist brightened as Jake walked in. Her face turned down when

Kayla appeared at Jake's side, close enough to be a warning to any intruders.

"Can I help you?" she asked, keeping her eyes on Jake.

My brother nodded and put the vial of zombie goop on the counter. Samantha, the receptionist, reacted better this time. She sighed and picked up a phone.

"Jerry? Sam. Mr. Talon just dropped off anther vial. Yes, it's contained. Okay, I will." Sam hung up the phone and opened a drawer, pulling out a heavy plastic container. She used her pen to move the vial into the bin and sealed it with a lid. It was a bit of a letdown, since the last time we were here, they all freaked out on us.

Samantha turned to Jake. "Anything else?"

Jake shook his head, but I was curious about one thing. I stepped up to the counter beside Jake.

"Hey, Samantha? What's in those vials we brought? Just curious," I asked.

Sam smiled, happy to take her attention away from a non-responsive Jake and a glaring Kayla. "Couldn't say, but Jerry should be able to fill you in on that one. I can say that when he figured it out, he spent about an hour debriefing the president about it."

That sounded a little more serious. "Is Jerry coming up soon?" I asked.

Sam nodded. "He should be here any second."

"All right. I'll wait." I looked over at Jake and he arched an eyebrow in my direction. I didn't respond and he shrugged, moving outside with Kayla right behind. Julia looked at me and I nodded towards the door. She left with a curious glance backwards, but left it at that.

As soon as the outside door shut, Jerry arrived with another person in a long lab coat wearing heavy rubber gloves. The assistant picked up the container and walked back the way they had come. Jerry was about to leave with a small wave before I stopped him.

"Jerry? Aaron Talon. A moment, if you don't mind," I asked politely.

Jerry looked impatient, but since I made sure I looked like I was not about to be ignored, he decided it was better to talk and get it over with.

"Sure. What can I do for you?" He asked with forced patience.

"Only one question. What's in those vials we keep finding?" I figured since I was risking my life to stop its spread that I ought to know what I was dealing with.

Jerry shook his head. "Probably the worst thing you could imagine. Those vials contain mutated Enillo virus. It's worse than the original strain, and nearly airborne lethal. Someone went to a lot of trouble to put this together or they have a very fertile breeding ground for the virus."

I was a little confused. "Are they just harvesting zombies? That would make my search a little easier."

Jerry shook his head again. "No. What they are doing is taking healthy hosts, injecting them with the virus, and then pulling this out of their brain stems. The DNA we've looked at from the virus you've collected suggests the hosts are all about the same age, and the same gender.

I had a sinking feeling in my stomach that I wasn't going to like the next thing I heard. "So, what are you saying? Everyone in that host pool was specifically chosen?"

Jerry looked at the ceiling, then directly into my eyes. "If I had to guess, Mr. Talon, I'd say if you found the source of this material, you would also find the whereabouts of our kidnap victims."

CHAPTER 29

"Don't be shy, I know you're there."

Shuffle shuffle moan.

"Come on, baby, it will be quick, I promise."

Shuffle shuffle.

"Just give me something to work with, no reason to be afraid."

Shuffle.

"There you go, that's my girl. Was that so hard?"

Moan, moan. **Bang!**

I fired my rifle, sending a .30 caliber bullet hurtling towards the zombie I had been stalking for ten minutes. The heavy bullet passed through her as if she wasn't there, but the shock wave blew her head apart like a popping balloon. One second it was there and the next it was gone. Pretty spectacular if you were just observing from the sidelines. I was observing through the scope, and it was just gross. Her body fell backwards and wedged itself between two cars, destined to rot away like so many others.

We'd been at this for the better part of the morning, and it was one big mess of misery. The highway of I-57 had been compromised, and it wasn't a thrill to begin with. The zombies that had previously been contained in their cars had been loosed and they were wandering free along the road. Three barriers had been removed from exits, and to make the cake even sweeter, it looked like the barricade to the city had been compromised. A steady stream of very nasty looking zombies was headed our way.

I should say, *my* way. Jake had taken charge of the situation, sending Julia and Kayla to hunt down the free-range zombies while he took care of re-blocking the roadway and finding additional help to deal with roamers. I got the job of finishing off the zombies that were left on the road, and to close off the city, once more.

Jake made the job sound easy. "Just close the doors to the cars, kill the ones out on the road, and you're good."

I initially thought it was going to be easy, partially because I wanted to believe Jake, but mostly because I was an idiot. The first couple of miles were easy, just strolling down the center of the lanes, kicking or pushing doors shut, and shooting the occasional zombie. No worries, right?

Then things began to change. The zombies that were still on the road were not the recently infected kind. They had been in hot and cold cars for over twenty years. They had evolved in that time and were smarter than your average convert was. They were weak as kittens, though, and their skulls were more brittle than the newer models, but they were still deadly for all that. Most of them were black with rot and mold, and several were missing fingers, hands, or even jaws. Those were my special, favorite nightmare.

For every one I killed, I thought of new and painful ways I was going to thank Jake for this lovely assignment. I just hoped Julia and Kayla were doing all right.

The last one I shot had actually moved in between the stacked cars and had been trying to wait for me to get closer so she could grab me. I had moved to the other side of the road and let her hunger get the better of her. When she looked out to see where I was, I blew her head apart.

I wasn't shy about ammo, having been replenished by the capital recently. They had sent teams out once upon a time to find whatever they could, and other had gone to the ammo manufacturing plants. I could care less as long as they were giving it to me to use.

I walked on, with the rising sun filtering through the stacked cars and their windows, throwing weird light patterns all over the place. I passed through a small canyon of rust and death, with the light and shadows making it seem like I was underwater. Hidden in the crevasses were dark things and monsters.

Another five miles brought me seven more kills, and I stepped up to an overpass. I couldn't see through the cars, and I wanted to look out, so I figured it would be a good idea to go climb to the top of the cars. I got the crazy notion I could do some long range sniping up there and save myself the trouble of dealing with the nasties closer up. I opened the door to the bottom car, wrenching it through the rust that had accumulated. Standing with one foot on the seat and the other on the door in the open window, I reached up and jerked on the handle to the door on the second car up. I thought to climb up and at least get on the hood of the car.

What I didn't think about was having a zombie be attached to the door I jerked open. It fell past me with a barely audible groan and landed in a heap on the ground.

"Jesus!" I was startled enough that I let go of the door and tried to jump away from the ghoul beneath me that was slowly getting up. Unfortunately, the door I was standing on swung as doors are supposed to do, and my left foot moved way past comfortable and into painful, when I suddenly tried to figure out how far my legs could spread. I didn't want to think about the zombie standing up and having its teeth level with my crotch, so I kicked off with my other foot and landed on my ass right in front of the zombie, one leg on either side of its widening maw.

I scrambled backwards, trying to get a weapon in front of me, but the zombie caught my attention in the most uncomfortable way. It reached out with a skeletal hand and grabbed the fly area of my pants.

"Gaaaahh!" I yelled, crabbing backwards and dragging a zombie with me. I had one chance to save myself, and I kept moving backwards to keep that chance. The zombie helped as an incentive, as it raised its blacked head and teeth in a grotesque feeding pose. I moved with one arm and two legs, trying to draw my pistol to kill this thing clamping on my crotch. Its grip was uncharacteristically strong, and I don't think I have met a more determined dead thing.

I finally got my gun out, and as I brought the weapon to bear, the zombie snapped its head forward, chipping its teeth on the gun. That was the last thing it did in this world. The bullet blew its tonsils out the back of its head, and took a good chunk of its brain with it.

I lay there for a moment, just me, my gun, and a dead zombie with its hand still gripping my crotch. I reflected religiously for a moment, thanking God no one had seen what had just happened.

CHAPTER 30

I got up and shook my head at what might have been, breaking into a small sweat as I did so. I'm not sure what worried me more; having a zombie bite me in the groin or having Jake watch me deal with it and never letting me forget the incident for the rest of my life.

I looked back up at the pile of cars and decided it wasn't worth it. My luck was done with that little adventure. I stayed on the ground and decided to walk the rest of the way to the main barrier, dealing with the zombies as they came. From my momentary vantage point, it didn't look like there were too many left. Most of them had passed and they were being hunted down by Jake and the women.

As I walked forward, I closed car doors and truck doors, losing count as I passed one hundred. Someone was not playing fair by trying this nonsense. These zombies had a long time to smarten up, and they were much cleverer than a newer zombie, relatively speaking. It was like comparing a frog to a mouse. A frog just was, while a mouse had the ability to figure things out.

I shot a few with my rifle, the big gun's blasts echoing in the small canyon of rust and rubber. I was using an M1A, like the one my dad used to good effect a long time ago. He left his in the Potomac in DC; I found mine on a trip south when we were collecting. It was powerful, reliable, accurate, and it held a lot of bullets. In zombie hunter language: perfect. I wasn't worried about anything behind me, since I had killed everything, and I was trying to draw out the ones who were wandering about and put them down. A couple of them tried to play hide and seek, but the heavy bullets found them through fenders and doorframes.

About two miles up the road, and a few dozen dead zombies, I finally reached the barrier to the rest of the highway heading north. As I looked it over, I realized how simple a solution it was to a complicated problem. How do you keep potentially thousands of zombies from crashing free of their highway prison and seriously ruining your day? You use what's on hand. Thankfully, at the time, Illinois highways were in a constant state of repair. As such, there were concrete barricades all over the place. Four strong men could easily lift one, and the little holes on the bottom made it simpler to stack using wooden poles to lift. Three of them made a barrier nine feet high. Stack them lengthwise on the highway, and they become a blockade of concrete six feet thick. The zombies weren't getting through without help.

As I approached the barrier, I saw that these particular zombies had received exactly that. The far left side had been shifted, not far enough to allow more than one zombie through at a time, thankfully, but I could see where men had worked on making a passageway. I was going to have a time trying to fix this myself.

However, that would have to wait a minute. Right now, a very horrid looking zombie was making his way through the opening, leaving long dark streaks on either side as he oozed his way closer. His single eye was focused on me and no little thing like stonework was going to stop him. I was about to shoot him when I realized I ran the risk of a ricochet coming back and messing up my pristine person. That would never do. I put my rifle down on the hood of a car that looked like it might have been expensive in its day and turned my attention back to my squeezing, struggling friend. He was about free of the barrier and reached out with a skeletal hand to make a grab at me.

I knocked away his hand and rewarded all of his hard work with a spike to his head. He fell down and wedged himself firmly between the barricades, blocking the passage until another managed to figure out how to climb over his body. As I watched, that was immediately happening. Another zombie, a female this time, was sliding through the barriers, keeping her eyes on me as she groaned slightly and started to claw her way over her dead companion. Behind her, I could see a small group of dead gathering to take their turn at the newly opened pathway.

"Not today, sweetheart," I said as I planted my tomahawk between her eyebrows. She fell on top of the first and another was making its way to join the other two. I started to think I could be here for a long time unless I managed to have a more permanent solution that didn't involve me dying.

I killed a third and a fourth, and the corpse barrier made a good blockade for a short amount of time, but I needed something solid they couldn't climb. I knew I couldn't lift a concrete barricade on my own, but I knew I could leverage one if I could get up on top. I went to the other side of the barrier and climbed up, straddling two of them as I looked out towards the city. The highway was a mass jumble of cars, zombies, and skeletons. Just a little way ahead of me was the city wall, the only thing keeping back a few million zombies still roaming the city limits of Chicago. I couldn't imagine what it must have been like in the early days of the Upheaval, with everyone trying to escape the carnage behind them, only to find it travelling the road with them. How many souls had been lost just on the highways God alone knew.

I went over to the moved barricades and pushed on the top one. It moved slightly, so I wedged myself between it and the one next to it. It was heavy, but with a good deal of pushing and a whole lot of cursing, I pushed it over to fall on the zombies below. Four dead zombies were no match for three hundred pounds of falling concrete, and zombie goo squirted out across the road as the stone fell. I got up and went to the next barricade, pushing it over with new and invented curse words. The added weight and height stopped all zombie traffic, and I think a few zombie organs blew out across the highway to add to the mess I had made.

The activity drew the attention of hundreds of zombies, and there was a drift in my direction. I waited to see if the new barricade would hold, and when it did, I just shook my head at the crowd. Some of them looked back at me with what seemed to be some kind of emotion, and it was a little unsettling. I knew they could evolve and become problem solvers, and the little ones were deadly if left alone for too long. However, I got the feeling that some of these zombies were disappointed they couldn't step and be killed.

I shook the feeling off and took a minute to wipe my tomahawk. Then I shouldered my rifle and headed back the way I came. I had a good walk ahead of me, since Jake had taken the truck and went off to the south somewhere to kill zombies. I found it a little ironic that I was surrounded by cars yet I still needed a ride.

CHAPTER 31

I passed my crotch grabbing nemesis after a time and shuddered again at the thought of what might have been. I wondered what people did in the old days when there were literally thousands of zombies grabbing at you and trying to bite off whatever they could reach. Probably, they just died and went to go grab someone for themselves.

Three miles down the road, I reached the spot where I had joined the fun. Jake had relocked the gate and I considered getting off the road when I decided to keep going a little further down. If they job was done here, then I had a better chance of finding them south of here.

At the next exit, I left the highway and walked steadily. I hoped to find someone who could point me in the direction of the capital, but as I read the faded signs off the highway, I realized where I was and how much farther I had to go. I also began to harbor the sneaking suspicion that Jake had given me the rotten job on purpose and left me as some sort of lesson. I figured I'd settle his ass soon enough.

South of my exit took me into some run-down areas, and I kept my rifle ready and my eyes on the lookout. The houses were close together, although I doubted anyone lived here. The homes were all of the same type, two story brick and built barely three feet from its neighbors. Open doors and broken windows told the tale as clearly as a sign, and I didn't bother to look into any of them. I was a little surprised they were still standing, as my father had normally destroyed useless or zombie occupied buildings. However, as I stood on a little hill and looked out over the community, I realized how many homes there were and how impossible the job would have been.

Back in the day, there must have been a lot of humans around.

The sun was approaching noon, and I kept moving south. I knew that I would eventually reach the canal, and that could get me to the capital in relative comfort if I could find a boat or canoe. Once there, I could easily await the return of my companions. The more I thought about it, the more appealing it became. I would get another hotel room, order up some good food, and await my battered and bruised crew. After a comforting shower with Julia, we could settle down and enjoy each other's company all night long.

I was grinning like an idiot with these thoughts when I walked right into an ambush.

CHAPTER 32

"Nice gear." A voice penetrated the fog of my mind and I looked around to see myself surrounded by five men of various sizes and shapes. The two behind me pointed shotguns at my head, while the three in front and to my sides held rifles and clubs. Their gear was old but well cared for, and they did not have the look of hungry scavengers. These looked like hunters, individuals sent out by a headman to find what they could and take what they wanted. Stupid, horny me walked right up into them.

I overcame my surprise quickly enough to answer. "Thanks, I like it myself. What can I do for you?"

One of the men behind me snickered and I spared him and his friend a small glance out of the corner of my eye. I was in a bad way and I knew it. These weren't your run of the mill townies who thought they might try their hand at a little pilgrim robbery. No, these guys lived on the fringe, and I thought it likely they made regular runs to the city for items to sell either at the capital or other established communities. They were brave, tough, and likely skilled, so I was going to have to tread carefully.

"You guys collectors?" I asked, keeping my hand on my rifle. I didn't see any signs of tension on the hands holding the guns, so I stopped being nervous about someone accidentally shooting me in the head. On the other hand, calm cool and collected meant they had done this enough times before that they were not too worried about the outcome. Whether or not I lived was a side effect.

"Going after other people's shit is for idiots, man, don't waste my time." The speaker was a mid-sized young man, probably my age, with hard eyes and a sneer that never seemed to end. His clothes were an interesting collection of colors and patterns, making me wonder about the quality of his eyesight.

"Where you going, man? Most people don't stray unless they got backup somewhere." His eyes flickered around quickly before they settled on me again. I tensed slightly, but my window was gone before I had a chance to move.

"Just came off the highway, closing the barricade. Somebody opened the route to the city. Was it you?" I asked, shifting my stance slightly. I hoped to put them off balance by taking control of the conversation.

The sneering man shook his head. "Zombie come, zombie go. Ain't no never mind to me. You, on the other hand, interest me."

"How so? I've never been interesting before. Do tell." I shifted again, casually turning a little to my left. The barrel of my rifle was now closer to the men behind me, without being too obvious about it.

The man holstered his weapon. "You're not begging for your life, and you ain't offering us everything to let you go without hurting you. Unless I miss my guess, you're about to do some serious violence if we don't turn out just right."

I smiled as I heard the tightening of grips on guns behind me. "Absolutely. And holstering your gun wouldn't spare you. I'd still shoot you dead, armed or not. The only real chance you had was shooting me from ambush, which you chose not to do. Thanks for that, by the way." I took a chance and glared at the men around me. "Even without guns, I'd still kill you all. Just so we understand each other."

The man smiled back and lowered his head slightly. He then raised his left hand and made a circular motion. The men behind me walked wide and fell in as the men walked away. After twenty yards, he called out.

"Mind telling me your name. I might need to explain why I'm walking away," he said.

"Aaron. Aaron Talon," I said, feeling cocky.

The man thought a minute. "Seems like I might have heard of you. Good luck with your walk."

I gave him a salute and kept on the road, walking until I got out of sight. Once I passed their vision, I broke into a fast run and held it as long as I could. I ran under train bridges and out towards a wide canal. I knew that canal as well as I knew my own name. It connected with another canal which would take me to the city if I wanted to, or I could make it back to the capital, which I know I hoped I would see again. I don't know whom Sneering Man might be working with, but I knew they weren't just going to let me go if I could help it. The more I thought about it, the more I realized how stupid I was to tell him my name. Arrogance is a virus almost as bad as the Enillo.

The only hope I had was to take path they didn't expect, and maybe get outside their area of control. If they came at me then, the odds were higher in my favor. Never fight on the ground of your enemy's choosing, as Uncle Tommy used to say.

At the rickety bridge spanning the canal, I crossed quickly, and then dove into the heavy brush on the edge of the water. The area was dark and forbidding, but I knew the outside was the only real thick part. Inside, the sun didn't reach all that often and there was a surprisingly large amount of space to move. I ran quickly, trying to be as quiet as possible, skipping over deadfalls and leaves. Years of falling leaves and decay made a ground that was soft and quiet. The canal lapped noisily at its banks, helping to mask my movement. I walked more than I ran, but I lengthened my stride to compensate. I was trying to avoid tripping on anything, and I hoped I was swift enough that any animals that might run and give away my position would be too startled to do anything until I was past.

I counted my steps as I moved, and after five hundred, I stopped to listen. I closed my eyes and filtered out the normal sounds, concentrating on the sounds that shouldn't be there. A car door closing, a slap of leather against wood, the metallic chambering of a round into a firearm. All of this came to me from the direction I had fled and from directly south of me.

Uncle Charlie had taught me that patience was the ability to control your natural tendencies to make and idiot out of yourself. I had already done half of that, so I figured to make up for it by seeing how I can turn this situation around. I had good cover with the trees, and I had a good point of retreat in the canal if I needed it. I didn't relish the idea of getting wet, but I would do what I had to. In this case, I would take a page from Dad's book. *You want me; you're going to earn it.*

CHAPTER 33

I rummaged in my pack until I found the little leather cap I kept to put over the muzzle of my rifle. It kept out dirt and debris, but I could shoot through if I had to. Attaching that little bag, I slung my rifle across my back at a slant, able to slip it under my right arm and fire from the hip if needed. Between my rifle and my sword, I had a big X on my back, and I didn't even think about what that meant.

Going back to the water's edge, I stuck my hand in the black mud streaked my face with it, breaking up the whiteness of my skin and giving it a pattern to blend in with the sun spotted darkness under the canopy of the trees.

Drawing my tomahawk and my grandfather's knife, I slipped through the woods as quiet as the morning mist. Behind me, I could hear several shouts as men were unsuccessful in figuring out where I had disappeared. I knew it wouldn't last, but they would regret finding me.

I kept moving to the west, following the river. I didn't know if they were going to get ahead of me or if they were going to get lazy and give up after a time. I wasn't going to chance that they were just out for my well-being and wanted to give me directions. A road followed the river, but since it hadn't been used in a long time, it wasn't in great shape. If they were going to pursue me on that, their vehicles were going to take a hell of a beating. Midwestern winters were difficult on roads when there wasn't anyone around to take care of them.

Every fifty yards I stopped to listen. That was Uncle Charlie's trick. "Nature knows more than you do, boy, so listen to what she's telling you. More importantly, listen to what she's not telling you." It took me a while to figure that one out, but he meant that it was just as important to understand the things I was supposed to be hearing but wasn't. Bugs that suddenly went quiet and squirrels that reversed direction for no known reason were all signs of something out of kilter.

Three people were in the woods behind me that I was sure of. Ahead of me, I didn't hear anything, and to the side I could hear a truck laboring along the road. Again, I cursed myself silently for being stupid enough to give my name. Next time, I'll give Jake's and just force the fight right then.

As I moved, I tried to stay quiet and disturb as little as possible. If the men behind me were skilled trackers, then I didn't want to give them a map to follow. I could be in for a long chase.

Suddenly, I froze. Up ahead was a small clearing, with a little brick building next to the edge of the canal. It looked like a very small house, about the size of a garage. It had a corrugated metal roof and a tall tower reaching up from the northwest corner. The windows had been broken and it looked like it hadn't seen anyone in years, but as I checked it out I thought it might make a decent place to make a stand.

That is, if I was going to be stupid twice. This place was a trap, but it could be useful. I sprinted across the opening and tried the door. The grey metal was rusted in a dozen places but it opened. Inside the house was a table, a chair, some wires sticking out of the wall, and a well-looted kitchenette. Four windows let in a lot of light, and there wasn't anything else to see, except this place was completely indefensible. But I got an idea, and moved fast. I drew the curtains across the windows facing the brush I had just left, and then got out of the building. I stood just outside the open door and waited until I heard some movement in the trees. I stuck my rifle through the front window and kicked the metal door shut. I fired three times through the building, my bullets passing through the dusty curtain on the other side.

I didn't wait to see what happened as I turned and bolted for the trees. I ducked into heavy growth and stopped, not wanting to give my position away by running like a fool. I replaced the leather cap on my rifle and waited to see if my ruse had worked.

CHAPTER 34

Across the clearing, a lone man appeared by the river's edge, low to the ground and trying to stay out of the line of fire afforded by the windows. He held his rifle up and when he had a clear shot, he ran towards the building. Stopping there, he signaled to the woods and two others appeared and made their way to the same place. I could see a brief discussion going on, and they finally stormed the house, going in the front door effectively and quickly. They obviously had done this sort of thing before as a team. They didn't get in each other's field of fire, and they moved in a coordinated fashion.

As soon as the men went in the house, I slipped back into the woods and put another two hundred yards between me and the house. I stopped when I heard a truck approaching. It sounded very heavy and powerful, not your ordinary truck. I could hear doors slam as people got out, and a voice reached my hiding spot.

"Why are you out here? Is he dead in there? We heard shots."

Another voice, probably from one of my pursuers, answered. "No, it's empty. He must have fired and then ran. We've wasted time here."

The first voice laughed, and it was a nasty sound. "Yes, you have, and nothing to show for it. You had Aaron Talon in your grasp and you fucked it up. He's probably watching us right now, laughing at the fools we're making of ourselves." The voice turned mean. "Find him or I'll kill you. If you screw up, you'd be better off shooting yourself. I catch you, and you'll wish you had."

I didn't hear anything else, as I left the area in as much of a hurry as I dared. I had no idea who might want me so badly, but as I ran, I went through in my head the number of people who might. The only face that kept coming up was the white-haired man I had words with a little while ago. I had a gut feeling about him and it wasn't good.

If the men he was commanding were worried about failure, then they were going to be right on my tail. I had bought myself a decent head start, but I didn't think it was going to last. The last thing I wanted was to bring this trouble to Jake or Julia, so I was going to have to deal with it here. I went over to the canal and stowed my rifle in the crook of a tree. Unless they were looking up and walking backwards, they weren't going to see it.

I moved further up the waterway and found a tree that hung out over the water. After I cleared the brush and rocks from the base, I climbed two short branches until I was about six feet off the ground. I put my knife in my right hand and my tomahawk in the other. I had to wait to see how they approached before I made my move. I was going up against three trained men carrying rifles. The only advantage I had was surprise.

Fifteen minutes later, I heard walking. They were moving quickly, not bothering to be silent. I guessed they assumed the advantage in numbers. They were spaced about thirty feet apart, which made sense if they were being shot at, but I had no intention of announcing myself like that.

They passed my tree and when they were about ten yards away, I dropped soundlessly to the ground, landing on my cleared spot. I took off at a small run, trying to match my steps with theirs, only faster.

I reached the first man in a couple of seconds, and without breaking stride, I stabbed him in the back of his neck. Three inches of steel came out beneath his Adam's apple, which silenced and killed him.

I didn't wait for him to drop, I turned and ran towards the next man, who was unaware his companion was down on the ground, drowning in his own blood, unable to move thanks to a severed spine. I switched my tomahawk to my other hand, having left my knife in the next of the first man. I swept towards the second man and he actually turned his head, alerted by my movement in his peripheral vision.

Unfortunately, for him, it was the spike end of my tomahawk, which caught him right between his very wide eyes. He died with one of the stupidest looks on his face that I had seen so far. I left the weapon and moved to the last man, swinging slightly back to stay out of his sight.

I pulled my other knife and moved in, readying to kill him as I had the first man. I was three steps away when he suddenly turned around, looking for his companions. He looked my way and opened his mouth, to either scream or shout, trying to bring his rifle up.

I imagine I was a bit of a sight, with my wild man makeup and glittering blade reaching out to try and take his life. He got his gun halfway around when I plowed into him, slamming him backwards into a tree. His gun flew out of his hands and he dropped to the ground on his rear. I had to give him credit; he was a fighter. He tried to pull his pistol, but I kicked it away when it cleared its holster. He then tried to pull a knife, but dropped it when the tip of my knife pricked the underside of his chin. I had his full and undivided attention from there on out.

"Hands out, hug the tree behind you. Move or shout and you're dead. Nod if you understand," I said, shifting the knife to a point just behind his jaw and under his earlobe. It was a very uncomfortable place to have a knife. You couldn't get out of the way without injury, even in the best of circumstances.

The man slapped bark and nodded vigorously, wincing a little as the knife tip bit him and started a thin line of blood running down his neck. I smiled slightly, knowing my painted face made it look a lot worse.

"Why does Ben want me?" I asked, playing a hunch.

The man shrugged as best he could. "You humiliated him, and you're interfering with his plans. He'll never forgive you for hitting him and taking his gun."

I said nothing, but inside I was cursing myself silly. If I had known the trouble that little old man was going to cause, I would have squeezed the life out of him right when I had the chance.

"Why is he trying to restart the Upheaval? What's his end game?" I asked, playing another hunch.

"Don't know anything about that. I just know he hates you and your brother, and he has plans for your girlfriend." The man grinned. "I heard she's a real looker, too."

I cocked my head at him. "Why would you try and commit suicide like that?"

The man shrugged again. "I can't go back without you, and Ben doesn't reward failure. I'm dead if I try to run, so you may as well finish the job."

I looked at him for a long moment before deciding what to do. I couldn't tell if the man was bluffing or not. I decided to end the suspense.

"Okay," I said, jamming the knife blade deep into his skull, killing him immediately. He died with a very surprised look on his face. I didn't want another enemy to look out for, so any thoughts I may have had about letting him live had gone straight into the canal.

I needed to send a message though, so I retrieved my weapons and collected the firepower of my pursuers. One of them had a really nice Winchester rifle that I thought Jake would like. He always liked westerns for reading.

The thought of westerns gave me an idea. I pulled the bodies out to the old road and using some lengths of rope, I hung them from three different trees. After they were up there, I spayed them with a little kerosene and set them on fire. I figured the smoke and smell ought to send some attention their way. I wanted to send a very powerful message.

Hunt me, and you'd better be ready to go all the way.

CHAPTER 35

I kept walking, following the canal. I knew where it was going, and I held out the hope that I might find some kind of boat which would get me to the capital sometime in the near future.

I passed under one of the big highways that my dad used to talk about. He said they were the biggest reason so many people died. Back in the day, people relied on their cars for everything, and when the end came, they thought their cars could get them to safety. Dad figured, if they all stayed put, hunkered down for a week or two, then a lot of people might not have died and the world might not have ended. Who knows?

As I walked, I noticed the vegetation getting a little thin on the land side. I wasn't too familiar with this area, so I poked my head through the brush. I was surprised to see there was a serviceable road running along the same direction as the canal. I wasn't one to ask a gift horse to open wide. If there was a decent path to take that kept me from slugging it out with brush and mud, I was all for it.

I walked cautiously, making sure to keep quiet though the area had long been overrun and abandoned. I could see a few tendrils of smoke from cooking fires here and there, which told me at least a few people were trying to make a go of it away from towns.

I was just past a road called Ridgeland when I began to hear things that were out of place. I expected some noise, and was fully prepared to dismiss what could be considered working routine noises. However, a chorus of groans and a scream, followed by some more groans was something else entirely.

I listened for a second to get my bearings, and then headed to the remnants of a subdivision across the way. I slipped over a fence and went through a backyard, stepping over a small plastic pool, which I swore was in nearly every yard I ever visited. A sandbox in the corner had a small tree growing out of it, and the ground near the house crunched as I went past. A look down revealed a glittering trove of broken glass. The house had nearly every window broken out. I looked over the edge of the fence I went through and listened again, focusing on the sounds and zeroing in on the location. It seemed to be coming from a little further south.

I flicked the safety off on my rifle and jogged across the street, moving around the burned out remains of several houses. Once I reached the back, I could see where the problem was. On the edge of a cul-de-sac, a house was surrounded by about twenty zombies. They were dark enough in color to make me think they were originals, and I wondered briefly, where the heck they came from this far south from the city and highway.

However, another scream pushed me into action and I ran into the middle of the cul-de-sac bringing my rifle up as I did so. I didn't have much of a plan except just kill the dead guys. I fired three times, killing two of them and causing everyone to look my way. I didn't wave; I just fired again, killing another one. After that, it was going to become a free for all, except a voice cut through the groans.

"Please save our daughter! We've been bitten and we can't hold off the ones in the house much longer. The virus is making us weak! My wife is down already!" A man waved from a second story window, and I could see, even at that distance, his arms were bloody and torn. Another scream came from the house and he ducked back inside.

Damn. There were about ten zombies between the house and me. Who knows how many more were inside. To make matters worse, I couldn't shoot towards the house anymore, since I didn't know where the girl was. .308 bullets didn't give much thought to houses as they generally passed right through them. I had to get past this bunch and get to the house, or things were going to get ugly. I put my rifle back over my shoulder and pulled out my sword. If it had been two or three ghouls, I would have used my 'hawk, but anything over five go to the attention of the big cutter.

I didn't wait for the zombies to come at me. I ran at the first one and cut him down, hacking his head in half. I used the momentum of the swing to cleave the skull of another in two, and after I pulled the blade out of his face, used the position to thrust the point into the eye of another. I had a little bit of wiggle room after that, and ran to the edge of the group that was trying to encircle me. I swung one-handed to bring down another, and the backhand swipe off that took out a fat little bastard with no nose.

I ducked under the grasp of a female that was a little quicker than the rest, slamming the edge into her temple and slicing the top half of her head off. It was ugly, but effective. The last four came at me as a group, and I decided to run around the cul-de-sac and spread them out. They couldn't all be the same speed.

As it turned out, they weren't. Two of them were faster than the others were and I ducked around a mailbox to put something in between us. One of the zombies walked right into it, knocking itself down. The other fell to my sword and the first died as he was trying to get up. The last two were easy pickings as they were slow and ungainly when trying to run me down.

I wiped off my blade and sheathed it, running over to the house. The man saw me coming and went back in, reappearing at the window holding a small girl, about seven years old. She looked terrified, and clung to her father. I couldn't hear what he was saying to her as he spoke his final words, but they were quick because he suddenly dropped her into my arms. I caught her easily and she covered her eyes with her hands. I looked up just as the man caught my eye and he was dragged back into the bedroom. There was a throaty roar and suddenly the window burst out as a zombie was thrown from the second floor. The man was certainly paying his way into the afterlife. I took a second to spray a little kerosene into the first floor window and light it. I hoped the house would catch and the rest of the zombies inside would get caught.

CHAPTER 36

The girl took her hands away from her face for a second and looked up at me with big brown eyes. She looked terrified, and I realized I hadn't cleaned the mud off of my face. I must have looked like hell. I tried to be reassuring

"Don't you worry, sweetheart. My name is Aaron, and I'm going to take you somewhere safe. Is that okay?" I said, hurrying away from the house.

The little girl nodded and curled herself into a small bundle, no doubt trying to wipe from her mind the last couple of hours of hell. I was still curious as to where that many zombies had come from. I would have heard of an outbreak like that, especially with some original zombies. As we walked, a lone zombie stumbled out the back door of the school, tripped over the threshold and smacked its head on the concrete. It lay still so I called that one a win and kept moving.

Suddenly, it made sense. The father had probably moved into the home because of the open land behind it, and one day he went to see if anything was in the school that he could use, never knowing there was a small horde of zombies that had been dormant for years. That happened from time to time as new areas were opened up and old zombies came out to play.

I walked along, making my way back to the canal as best I could. I knew I couldn't carry this girl all the way back to the capital, so I really was going to have to find some kind of transportation now. The girl didn't say anything, and when I looked down, she had closed her eyes. I figured she'd have to be exhausted, given what she had been through.

The sun was getting to its zenith and I was getting tired. Carrying what was essentially fifty pounds of dead weight in front of me was starting to take a toll, and after a good hour of walking, I was getting tired. So it was with some relief I saw what looked like a small settlement built up along the canal. Several boats were docked along small makeshift piers, and I had renewed hope that I could secure at least passage to the capital, if not the purchase of a boat outright.

The road split the settlement in half, with several occupied homes in the old subdivision on the land side. On the water side, there was a small gathering of cottages, and two large buildings in the center. One looked like a tavern, with a wide porch and several tables inside that I could see from the road. Six or seven men were relaxing on the porch, while a serving girl came in and out of the front door. The other building looked to be some kind of trading post, with several recovered items for sale on its front area, and a quick peek inside the door showed quite a few items on tables and on shelves.

As I approached the tavern, one of the men on the porch got off to look me over, and I couldn't hear what he called over his shoulder, but it gathered a few people from the interior.

I was about twenty yards from the porch when I happened to look down at the girl I was carrying. I expected to find her still asleep. What I didn't expect was to find her staring up at me, with bloodshot and black-rimmed eyes.

When my gaze met hers, she bared her teeth at me and twisted suddenly, looking to sink her teeth into the flesh of my upper arm! I was literally hugging a child that had died in my arms and come back as a zombie.

"Shit!" I reacted by pure reflex. I dropped the girl, stepping back as she fell to the ground, her teeth snapping shut on empty air as she barely missed biting my bicep. I didn't give her a chance to recover, as the only way to deal with the little ones was to kill them as quickly as possible.

I stepped forward, kicking her off her hands as knees as she struggled to get her balance and stand up. I didn't stop there. When she was on her back, I stepped on her chest and held her to the ground as she grabbed and pulled at my leg. Her face was a mask of rage and pain as she futilely tried to bite my boot.

I pulled out my tomahawk and smacked her in the head with it. I must have been holding back for some reason, because it took me three strikes to kill the little monster.

I stepped off the girl and shook my head. All that fighting her father did for her was for nothing. I wondered how she caught the disease, and figured that maybe she had put it in her own eyes when she rubbed her father's blood into her face. It was sad, really. This one wouldn't ever get a chance to grow up, ever get a chance to play anymore, or ever get the chance to see the big cities and the capital.

I snapped out of my little daydream when a word penetrated my thoughts.

"Jesus."

CHAPTER 37

I looked up and saw about thirty people staring at me. Some had their hands over their mouths, some had a sad look on their faces, and some looked at me with open hostility. One man ducked inside and came out with a rifle, which he pointed right at me.

"Hands up, mister! I don't know what the hell is wrong with you, but you better drop that axe and get your hands up *now*!" The man yelled at me and I could see several other men starting to edge out over the road in an effort to try and surround me.

I looked down at the girl, then my 'hawk, which was dripping zombie brains and blood into the road. I couldn't help myself; the stress of the morning just came pouring out. I tilted my head back and just laughed. When I came back to earth, the men were closer, but stopped when I glared at them. I pointed to the girl with my axe.

"Relax, she turned into a zombie in my arms. I was trying to rescue her from an attack on her folks' place. She got infected somehow." I wiped my 'hawk off on the girl's clothing, and another person gasped.

At the word attack, several faces turned to each other and looked worried. I helped them along.

"About two miles back, there should be a house on fire. Guy living there opened up a school which had some sleepers in there. They took him out and his wife. He tossed this girl to me, not knowing she was sick. Believe me, if she was well, I'd be handing off a scared, tired little girl to one of you right now," I said, trying to keep the rising dread of another fight out of my voice.

"Can you prove she was infected?" The man with the rifle spoke, and I was glad to see he wasn't pointing the gun at me any more.

I thought about that for a moment. How would I prove she was a zombie? As she looked now, she just appeared to be sleeping, albeit with three large cuts in her skull. I looked at my hawk and then I got an idea.

"You all know the virus burns red, right?" I asked, getting several nods in reply from a few of the older patrons. "Okay, then let me torch my tomahawk, and you'll see the red flame." I sprayed some kerosene on the axe, noting as I did that my supply was getting dangerously low. I pulled out a match and lit the blade, seeing with some satisfaction that the flames burned bright red, even in the noon sun.

After that, everyone relaxed. I just shook my head at the whole situation, watched as the tavern patrons went back to their tables, and oversaw the loading of the zombie corpse onto a small cart to be buried out of town. Seven men with serious looks on their faces went off to the east to see if there were any more zombies to be killed from that morning massacre. I ignored the looks I got from the assembled settlement folks and wandered into the trading post.

Inside was like nothing I had seen before. A collection of junk, the likes of which I hadn't figured could be piled into one place were there. There was everything from sewing kits to guns, jewelry to books. Tools were piled in one end, while a selection of clothing covered another. Pots, pans, lamps, and artificial limbs hung from the ceiling. I had to duck under a canoe paddle to look over the assortment of knives and hatchets that covered the top of a glass display. Inside the display was a small assortment of toys and child games.

"Help you?"

One of the displays seemed to be speaking to me, although on closer inspection it turned out to be a small woman seated behind the counter. She looked to be anywhere from thirty to three hundred, and her eyes blinked twice at a time, when she bothered to blink. Her blue hair was tied back in a ponytail, and her black eyes looked as if they belonged on something that used to be living.

I straightened to my full height and her eyes expertly looked me over. They took in my clothes, my weapons, and I could see the calculations going on in her head as to how much I might have to spend. If I had to guess, she probably already knew how much money I had in my pouch.

I smiled slightly. "I need a refill of kerosene, if you have it, and the use of a boat to the capital."

Blue took my container and walked over to a plastic jug that held a clear liquid. Placing my bottle under the spigot, she expertly filled it without spilling a single drop.

She brought it back to me and placed it on the counter. "Two coppers. Don't have any boats to rent, but my son can take you for a small fee."

I paid the inflated price out of my vest pocket where I kept only my coppers. I did that so people wouldn't see if I had any more money. However, with this woman, I figured it was useless.

"How much?" I asked, bracing myself for the price.

"Two silvers. Beats walking," she added.

I shook my head. "I don't want to buy the boat; I just want to get to the capital."

"Two silvers and you're there. No silver and you can fight some more little girls." That line was delivered with a smirk and I almost fell for it.

"Better that than getting scalped in here. No thanks."

The woman got off her stool and put her hands on her hips. Her lean body was tense, and I knew she had gotten through the original Upheaval with her wits and her will to live. She could probably fight pretty well, too, something I really didn't want to get into.

"You calling me a thief?" She asked quietly.

I shook my head. "You haven't stolen from me, so I'm reserving judgment on that charge. But I'm not paying your rates because I think they're too high. You want to get into trouble because someone tells you the truth, then you've got a lot a fighting ahead of you. The stuff you have in here tells me you used to be a collector, and still go out from time to time. But somewhere along the line, you realized people would be willing to pay for just about anything from the old places, and you set up shop. But since you have a son, the raids are much closer to home. Am I right?"

The woman's mouth opened when I spoke, and all she could do was nod. I smiled and left the shop, figuring I had a decent walk ahead of me. I knew I would regret not spending the money on a simple ride, but I had my pride, and that was more important than how my feet were going to feel in a little while. At least I told myself that as I left the settlement.

CHAPTER 38

About an hour later, I stepped into another world. A huge forest stretched to the south of me, and across the river, I could see another large forest. The trees were large and well developed, telling me this area was forest even before the Upheaval.

As I walked along the road, I could hear little noises coming from the woods. The big trees stretched their canopies over the road, so it was shaded and dim where I walked. Out of the corner of my eye, I could see movement as something large tracked my progress. I immediately thought of the cougars we had at Starved Rock, and knew nothing here would be as friendly. Just for luck, I whipped up my rifle and fired three quick shots at the trees, the booming reports echoing across the river and down the road. Animals scattered in all directions, and whatever had been stalking me had gone to ground. I was happy.

Dusk began to make its presence known in various ways, and I really didn't want to get caught out after dark, especially in this area. I knew I was decently close to the capital, but I also knew I wasn't going to make it before dark. I walked until I reached another road, and decided to find a place to stay for the night. I didn't have much in the way of choices, there were dozens of torn up buildings and homes. I needed to find somewhere that still had intact windows, someplace that was free of intruders, and somewhere I could light a small fire. Lately, the nights had been getting downright cold.

Just as the sun slipped the horizon, I happened upon a place situated on the edge of a forest. I would have missed it if I hadn't nearly walked into the sign by the side of the road. It read Cook County Forest Preserve Watchman's House. It was a small ranch style house made of brick. It was tucked back nearly into the woods, and the preserve had made a good effort in reclaiming it. Trees grew right up to the house, and the weeds were tall enough to need walking around. I made my way up the old driveway and fought my way through the weeds to look in the windows of the house.

Nothing seemed out of place. Actually, it seemed very well kept and tidy. I went to the back door and tried it first, smiling as the door clicked open. Like a lot of places, the front door was typically locked, but the back door stayed open. I went inside and checked things out.

The place was dusty, but not nearly as much as I thought it should be. All the furniture was where it should be, and I couldn't see any signs of a hasty exit. The kitchen cupboards were all bare, as was the fridge, but I wouldn't have eaten anything from them anyway. I took a couple of pieces of small kindling from the box by the fireplace and started a small fire. There wasn't much wind outside, so I figured the smoke wouldn't alert too many people.

I stretched out in front of the small flames and closed my eyes, replaying the events of the day. I hoped Jake, Julia, and Kayla were okay, and I wondered if I would see them tomorrow. I reminded myself that I needed to get to the capital first. After a while, I drifted off to sleep.

Sometime in the night, I awoke. I sat up and listened; trying to figure out what it was that had bothered my subconscious enough that it had awakened me. After concentrating for about ten minutes, I rearranged my weapons a little and went back to sleep.

In the morning, I unpacked and repacked my bag, taking a minute to burn off any zombie residue from my blades and sword. I even roasted the sheaths a little to make sure there wasn't any of the virus lurking around where it didn't belong.

Finally, I geared up and left, closing the place up as tightly as I had found it. As I was leaving, I glanced down at the grass by the rear window. Superimposed over my own footprint was another, slightly larger.

I scowled as the implications hit me. Someone had been here last night. They had approached the house and looked in. I checked the ground carefully, trying to find other tracks, but it was as if they had floated in, looked in the window, and then floated away. A chill crept into down my neck and I wondered again about the ghosts that haunted all over these parts. I checked the loads on my rifle and pistol and headed west.

CHAPTER 39

A half day later, I was at the outskirts of the capital on the southern side. I was slightly amused at my course of travel. It took me past my father's old subdivision, past the business building where he had a base for a time, past the house where he discovered he wasn't alone in the world, and over the ditch, Uncle Charlie had dug so many years ago as a defense against the hordes. He'd probably shake his head at the irony of it all.

I walked down the hills, heading for the hotel on the riverfront. I didn't want anything more than a place to lie down, a hot shower, and a good meal. Check that, if Julia was in town, I wanted something else, first.

At the hotel, the manager recognized me and found me a room right away. I asked if any of my companions were here and he said he hadn't seen anyone. Unconcerned, I went to my room and took a good shower, cleaning off the fights of the previous days. I changed into clean clothes and sent my old clothes to be washed. For lack of a good reason not to, I put all my gear back on and went down to the street to get something to eat.

I wasn't interested in anything heavy, just a sandwich or something. I wandered down to the vendors and grabbed a chicken sandwich. Sitting on the edge of the main pier, I ate and contemplated what I had learned over the previous days. Obviously, Ben was still gunning for me, and was willing to cause another apocalypse to get it done. I didn't know where that was going to take me, but I knew for sure I had to do something soon. I had been playing defense long enough, and I hoped the hanging men were enough deterrence for the rest of his crew.

I was lost enough in my thoughts that it took a while for it to register in my head that there was something wrong in my vicinity. I looked to the left and saw there was no one walking along the river, even though it was a warm evening and the sun was starting to send multicolored shafts across a darkening sky. On my right, it was the same thing. I began to get that old familiar felling, and it was telling me one thing, and one thing only.

Move.

I wadded up the paper that held my sandwich and tossed it in the air above my head. As I did that, I slipped off the pier and onto the grassy, sandy land that led to the actual water of the canal. I knew that whoever was behind me would be distracted by the sight of something white sailing over my head, and when they refocused on me, I'd be gone. It was a neat little trick Jake taught me a while ago, and it worked well most of the time.

Today was one of those times. I ducked under the pier and ran quickly under the walkway before grabbing a support beam and bodily lifting myself up into the small space between the floor planks and the support joists. Anyone looking for me would have a tough time of it. On the other hand, if they found me, I had two options. Surrender, or die fighting. I wasn't fond of either, but here I was.

My efforts were not wasted. Above me, I heard the thump of several booted feet and a few exclamations of surprise.

"What the hell? He just disappeared!"

"Get over the side. He had to have dropped off down there!"

"Shit. Did you see he was fully armed?"

"Just get going. We'll call your mamma if you die."

A large man dropped into view, landing heavily on his feet. He was armed in the fashion of the president's bodyguards, and I was curious as to why he was calling. He looked around, heading out a bit into the grass, and then came back. While he was out in the weeds, I got out of my hidey-hole and waited for him to return.

"Captain! Captain!" The man called out.

"Speak up."

"He's not out in the grass, sir."

I took that moment to step out from the pillar I was hiding behind. I leveled a pistol at the man as his eyes got huge. I motioned for him to keep talking to his officer.

"Sir!" The man called again.

"Give me something, soldier," the officer in charge yelled. His voice was a little strained, as if a simple operation suddenly had become quite complicated.

"I found the man, sir," the soldier said.

Suddenly, the Captain was all ears. "Really, are you sure?"

"Yessir! He's under the walkway pointing a really big gun right at me!"

The captain immediately changed his tune. "Mr. Talon? We've been ordered by the president to escort you to his home. Please don't do anything rash."

"What's this about? Normally, he just sends a runner with a message." I was very curious about the escort. Either something serious was happening or I was in some very deep shit.

"He'll have to explain that to you, sir. Please come with us." The captain was being very polite, and I figured I hadn't done anything lately.

"Be right there." I holstered my weapon, much to the relief of the guard in the grass. I walked over to one of the numerous ladders along the river walk and climbed up.

At the top, I was immediately surrounded, and one man went to take my gun. I twisted his wrist into his chest, dropping him to the deck. Suddenly, several of the guards sprouted guns and they were all pointing at me.

"Just an escort, huh?" I sneered, keeping a lock on the wrist of the man on the ground. I wasn't amused.

"Stand down, all of you. Especially you." The captain aimed this at me and I arched an eyebrow at him.

"Do tell. I'm very interested in why I was supposed to be unarmed." I pushed down on the man's arm, bending his elbow and making him very uncomfortable. With a sweep of my hand, I could dislocate his shoulder. The man cried out and his comrades took a step forward.

"Mr. Talon! Release that man! I will not allow you to escalate a situation to violence! Do it now!" The man was very agitated.

I let go of the man and stood up, towering over the small captain of the guard. "I'm not the one pointing guns, asshole. If there's an escalation, it's on you." I stared at the three men in front on me and I swear one of them broke out in a sweat.

"Stand down, all of you." The captain waved a hand around and the men put the safety on their weapons. "Mr. Talon, you are a very known and capable man. Right now, the president needs to speak with you. That's all I know. I was told to bring you to him. Could we please get this over with before something happens?"

I shrugged, knowing he was right. I didn't need to be a dick myself, and I was acting like one. Truth was, I was venting a bit, since I still hadn't heard from Julia or Jake, or even Kayla, for that matter. Something was wrong; I could feel it.

CHAPTER 40

I walked with the escort, and no one tried to take my weapons away. We wandered up the streets to the hills where the presidential home was, and I was brought up to the porch. I nodded a hello to Roger, but he returned my nod with a blank stare. Something was really up, now I knew for sure.

I waited while the captain went in, and a minute later, I was brought inside. President Jackson was seated in his office behind his antique desk, looking the most official I had ever seen. In a chair in front of him sat a man whose face I couldn't see. I walked forward and sat down in the chair next to him, and managed to conceal my shock when it was none other than the sneering gent who asked my name the other day! This was getting weirder and weirder.

The president got the ball rolling. "Aaron, this is Kevin Mastro. He's a trader in a community a little closer to the city and..."

"We've met," I said, interrupting Jackson.

President Jackson squinted a little at Mastro. "I see. And could you tell me the details of this meeting?"

I sighed like it was not big deal, but I was spinning my thoughts like crazy trying to figure out what angle this guy was playing. Whatever it was, I was not going to make it easy. "Not much to tell. I took care of the breach problem on the highway corridor, and as I was making my way back, I ran into Mr. Mastro here. Along with a few of his friends. They were the ones pointing guns at me while we talked."

President Jackson looked over at Mastro, who was no longer sneering. "You neglected to mention that little tidbit in your desire to bring Mr. Talon up on charges of murder."

I had to hand it to Ben. When one thing didn't work, he tried another. I was really getting tired of these games, but I couldn't do anything about it now.

Kevin tried another tack. "I didn't mention it because nothing happened. We talked and parted ways. Later, he kills three of my associates and hangs them, setting their bodies on fire. Who does that?"

President Jackson looked over at me and I had the presence of mind to look disturbed. I had to play the game though. "Not this guy. I wish I knew what you're talking about. I hit the north side of the river and kept going. My ride left me behind."

Jackson looked at us both, and I started to get mad, like I was being called to my father's presence to confirm or deny I had anything to do with whatever happened to break. I pushed the issue to make it easier.

"Look, if I had torched three bodies, it would have depleted my kerosene supply." I pulled out the bottle, showing them that it was full. "Talk to anyone in town who sells kerosene. I haven't been to any of them. I just got here a little while ago." I hoped like hell Mastro didn't know about that trading post on the canal. If he did, I was screwed.

President Jackson looked at Mastro, who looked like he had just eaten something fuzzy. After a minute, he spoke.

"Looks like Aaron isn't the one who killed your associates. I'd say you need to get back to your area and start a search for whoever is stalking your men. I'll send a few men to help out; hopefully they can root out this murderer."

Mastro looked like he was going to give birth to kittens. "Thanks, but no thanks. We'll handle it. Sorry for the misunderstanding. I'll be going now."

He stood up to leave but Jackson's voice stopped him. "Next time, get your facts straight before you come to accuse a man who has been working diligently with the government to eliminate new threats to our nation's security. Mr. Talon has my confidence and trust. Good day."

Once Mastro had left, President Jackson looked me square in the eye. "Okay, now talk to me. Did you do what he says you did?"

I spent the next ten minutes outlining what had happened over the last two days. I didn't spare any details, and I openly admitted what I had done. If it was going to get me arrested, so be it.

President Jackson listened, and then spoke. "Well, I can't condemn you for defending yourself, considering those men were clearly hunting you. But I have to ask, why did you burn the bodies after you hung them? Especially since they were clearly dead? That seems a little out of the ordinary, even for you."

I shrugged. "I wanted the men who work for Ben to start wondering if working for him was worth it. Especially if he had enemies who were willing to do that to just the corpses."

Jackson laughed. "That would make me think twice, certainly. But why bother trying to get you arrested? What purpose would that serve?"

"I don't know. That's been troubling me since Mastro left. Ben doesn't seem to make a move without purpose, but this one has me stumped. It's almost like he wanted to keep me in one place for some reason."

"You might have the right of it. But why would you need to be stopped, even for a short while? What's the advantage to that? I'm actually nervous about finding the answer," President Jackson said.

I nodded. "So am I. I'm going to head out and see if I can't find my crew. Then we're going to pay Ben a personal visit."

The president looked surprised. "You know where they are? Why don't you let the army handle this?" He hesitated at my look. "Never mind. You're your father's son."

"Thanks. I'll let you know how it turns out. I've had enough of Ben's games, and his vendetta is annoying," I said, getting up to leave.

"Let me see you out. The captain of the guard would like to know if he's supposed to arrest you."

I nodded my thanks and as we stood, there was a commotion outside. Stepping out, I saw Kayla pushing her way past the gate guard, and running up to the porch.

"Aaron! Thank God! You've got to come with me!" She threw her arms around my waist and buried her head in my chest as a greeting.

I held her for a moment, but pulled her gently away to look her in the face.

"What's happened? What went wrong?" I looked her over and she seemed okay, but there was the beginning of a bruise near her left cheek.

"I'm fine! We got ambushed yesterday by a group of men after we had cleaned up the zombies. I got away, but Jake and Julia were captured! We have to do something!"

CHAPTER 41

I led Kayla to a chair, while President Jackson waved to a servant to bring water.

"Okay, tell me what happened." I was raging inside, but kept it together on the outside.

Kayla took a few breaths, tucked her hair behind her ears and started her story.

"We were doing fine with the zombies, once you stopped the flow. It was more of just tracking and finding the roamers that had wandered off. We had help from the towns nearby, so it almost became kind of a family event. Find-the-zombie and all that." Kayla smiled slightly at her description. "But as we were cleaning up, a man came up and told us there was a situation in the next town. We figured he was okay, didn't seem like there'd be a problem. So we drove in. There were a few zombies, and we took care of them pretty quickly. But when we looked for the guy who led us there, he was gone. Jake thought there was something wrong, so he told us to get in the truck and go. I made it there first and started the truck. Just as I did, about ten men came running around the buildings from all sides. Jake was taken down first, and I thought they were going to kill him, when someone yelled out that we had to be taken alive. Julia was grabbed by three men, but not before, she took one out. She's a fighter, that woman of yours." Kayla gave me a half smile.

My heart jumped to my throat at the thought of Julia in the hands of Ben, but I had to force it down to hear the rest.

"How did you get away?" I asked.

"I wasn't going to, but Jake yelled out for me to get away and to find you. That's when a man jumped to the truck and tried to hit me, but I shot him in the face and drove off." Kayla put her head in her hands and started to cry. "I should have stayed! Jake needed me and I left!"

I put a hand on her back, then gently pulled her face up and looked into her reddening eyes.

"You did exactly the right thing. If you had stayed and been captured, then it might have been days before I had found out what happened. Right now, your escaping throws a problem Ben's way. He has Jake and Julia, but he knows you escaped and he will figure you found me. That's why he sent his idiot Mastro to try to get me into jail for a few days, so I wouldn't be coming after him. But he's got it to worry about now."

I stood up. "Now he knows I'm coming for him, and he won't do anything to Jake and Julia, because they'll be his last bargaining chips if everything goes south."

I started for the door, but President Jackson stopped me.

"Wait a minute. Where are you going? If you know where they are, then just let me send in the troops to get your brother and girlfriend back," he said.

I shook my head. "This one's on me. If Ben wants me, he's going to get me. But by God, he sure as hell is going to wish he didn't!" I headed out the door with Kayla running up right behind me. President Jackson shrugged and picked up a phone to make a call.

"I'm coming with you." She held up a hand to stop my protest. "I will not let you rescue Jake and Julia without me. You're going for Julia, and I'm going for Jake. And don't act surprised. I know what Julia told you." Kayla stepped ahead of me, as I stood there with my mouth open for a second.

I closed it and remembered what I had to do. I needed a quick plan and a few supplies before I headed out. I figured to get going within the hour. Jake and Julia were likely just getting back to Ben's headquarters about now, and he was going to spend some time gloating and leering. However, he was not going to be happy with Kayla escaping, so I hoped he would spend time getting ready for my arrival. If he didn't, he was going to die even more slowly than what I already had planned for him.

I was already in most of my gear, so it took no time at all to get myself ready. Kayla was in most of hers, so we just went to the hotel to get my rifle and we were on our way. I stopped briefly at the armory to gather more ammo, and after that, we were headed east.

"Are you sure of where we are going?" Kayla asked as I sped out of town.

"Not yet, but I will in a few minutes," I said as I kept my eyes on the road. Sure enough, another vehicle was on the road, this one was a small truck. It was the same one I had seen before when I was running from Ben's men. If I had a million gold coins, I'd bet them all that Kevin Mastro was at the wheel.

As it turned out, there were two men in the truck. They glanced over as I passed them, then their looks turned to shock as I slammed my much bigger truck into them, shoving them off the road and into the ditch. I stopped the truck and got out, waving Kayla to get down. I jacked a round into my rifle and waited by the rear corner of the bed.

The driver tried to get the truck out of the ditch, but after a second, realized it was hopeless. The passenger door opened, and a man I hadn't seen before popped out with a gun in each hand. He oriented himself and swung both in my direction.

About halfway through his movement, I shot him square in the chest. The heavy bullet threw him backwards into the pickup, where he slammed into the door, slid down, and left a blood trail all the way.

Kevin Mastro was smarter. He raised both hands above his head and climbed as best he could out of the ditch. He looked at his companion and shook his head slightly.

"I told him you'd kill him, but he wanted to try it anyway," he said with a grin.

I kept the big gun trained on Kevin's head. "Easy way or hard way?" I asked.

Mastro gave me a half smile. "I'll take the easy way, thanks. Ben has his fortress at the old school on Maple in Blue Island. It's got its secrets, and you might regret finding out what they are." He stopped for a minute. "I didn't have anything to do with your brother, by the way." Kevin lowered his hands. "Anything else?"

"One second," I said. "Kayla! You recognize this guy?"

Kayla popped her head up and gave Mastro a long look. "No, he wasn't there. I'd remember that red shirt he's wearing."

I looked at Mastro. "Leave this state, right now. If I even suspect you are residing in a *neighboring* state, I'll finish you. Clear?"

Mastro shrugged. "If you take care of Ben, I have nothing to worry about. I've wanted to hit the southern states anyway." He reached into the truck and pulled out a pack, and started walking back to the capital. He'd catch a ride on a boat and be gone before the day was out.

I safed my rifle and got back in the truck. Kayla looked at me.

"What now?" She asked.

"Now we scout the enemy's fortress," I said, throwing the truck into gear.

"And then?"

"Then we finish this."

CHAPTER 42

I drove the truck easterly, keeping to roads that I knew paralleled the canal. I knew approximately, where I was going, but I would know more specifically once I got closer. I figured we'd be there just at evening, which suited me perfectly. Dusk was when the human eye had the most trouble adjusting between the light sky and the dark ground. Back in the day, it was the best time to move over open ground when zombies were around, because they had a hard time seeing you.

When we reached the woods near the canal, I pulled over and got my bearings. I figured we had a mile to go before we reached the bridge that crossed the canal, and I wanted to make sure we weren't seen. Pulling up in a big damn truck didn't accomplish anything on that end, so I thought we were far enough away to not be seen by any chance sentry.

I pulled all of my magazines and loaded every one to capacity, putting handfuls of extra cartridges in my vest pockets. My knives were sharp and my sword was keen. I stroked the blade of my 'hawk with a small sharpening stone until it had the edge I wanted. I put on my dark gloves and pulled out a balaclava to cover my head. If I had to approach in the dark, I wanted to be invisible.

Kayla prepared as well. Her blades were all very sharp, and she had a small Glock on her hip. Spare magazines rode in her other hip, and she carried a backpack with assorted goodies. Her melee weapon was a short spear, about four feet in length and sporting a double-edged blade about a foot long. There was a sheath for the spear that hung down her butt, and a small u-ring held it within easy reach over her right shoulder.

I gave her a rifle and four extra magazines, which she distributed around her chest. I chambered a round into my M1A and looked in askance at Kayla.

She nodded in reply to my unspoken question. We were ready to go.

The canal flowed silently beneath us as we crossed the old bridge. The dark beams creaked ever so softly in the dimming light, and here and there, I could see places where the asphalt had dropped into the canal below. Eventually the whole thing would collapse and getting through on a boat would be tough.

On the other side, the viaduct was just a black hole, but I knew it was an illusion. The small tunnel actually turned slightly to the right, so we were looking at a flat wall, which made it seem like a cave. When we reached the other side, I waited a second for my eyes to adjust, since we went from pretty dark to pretty light.

Up on the corner of Vermont and Maple stood an old school building. The doors and windows that I could see were all intact, and the large windows on the old gym were all covered in iron grates which had protected them from the wandering hordes. If the other doors were in the same shape, this place would have been a good shelter during the Upheaval.

On the other side of the street was a row of small homes, looted and abandoned. This town would have been hard hit due to its proximity to the highway and the train station up the road. We kept to the sidewalk, staying under the canopy of trees and shrubs. So far, it seemed like we had managed to approach unnoticed.

After another block, everything changed. From my position under the bushes, I could see a serious problem with approaching the fortress. The old school was surrounded by a ten-foot wall of debris. Everything within fifty yards of the school had been torn down and used as part of the fortification. I could see parts of shingles, some bricks, chairs and tables, and what looked like some desks. On top of the wall was a series of boards lashed together to form a walkway for sentries. Completely surrounding the outer wall was a field of smaller debris. Bricks, stones, and wood planks were scattered all over, creating a huge uneven surface. Any zombie approaching this place would likely fall himself to death on all of the rocks and boards. Anyone alive trying to breach this place would have to slow down considerably to avoid twisting an ankle or outright breaking a foot. That slower person would make a hell of a target.

"I'm going to scout a bit, and see what I can see," I whispered to Kayla. "Stay here and try to get a sense for how the sentries are situated."

Kayla didn't argue, she just nodded and stared back at the school. We hadn't seen any sentries so far, but that could change.

I slipped into the brush and worked my way silently around the building. From what I could see, it was roughly in the shape of an 'H'. There was a cleared space for vehicles in the front of the building, but a pair of concrete towers on the outside of a set of huge iron gates served very effectively against most threats both living and dead. I didn't see any easy way in. Even the trees had been cut back to make sure the area around the building was one big killing zone.

I made my way back to where Kayla was waiting. She was still staring at the building, but she acknowledged my approach with a small nod of her head.

"It's been quiet, but there seems to be some movement now," Kayla said, pointing at the building." Sure enough, men suddenly appeared on the walkways, and took up stations at each corner of the wall. Two more men appeared in the towers next to the gates. If the fortress was hard to penetrate before, it suddenly became impossible.

"Damn," I said. "I don't know how the hell we can pull this off with these guys out there." I thought for a minute, and then made the hardest decision I hoped never to make. "We're going to have to back off and think this one through. We could snipe at last two of them, but that might get Jake and Julia killed in reprisal. We need to find a way to approach this place in the time when we can get in and get things done without too much risk to those two."

Kayla stared at me for a minute, and then looked back at the fortress. I could see she was in as much turmoil as I was. Inside I wanted to charge the gate, guns blazing, but without a reasonable way inside, it was suicide.

"Come on, let's back off and get further away," I said, moving through the brush. I was quieter now, and for some reason I stopped. I motioned Kayla to stop and I just sat with my eyes closed for a second. I thought I heard something, something out of the ordinary, but it didn't repeat itself, so I motioned Kayla to follow.

CHAPTER 43

Once out of sight of the fortress, we made our way back to the other school. A quick look around found the doors and windows were intact, and everything was locked. On the south end, a window unit air conditioner that I could reach by standing on the railing was outside the front door. With Kayla holding my legs, I managed to push the unit inside and pull myself in.

I found myself in a small office, with a fake wood desk and computer table taking up nearly half the space. A closet with no door was in front of me, and I could barely make out the school supplies stored there. I stepped through a smaller office that consisted of a desk and a computer taking up ninety percent of the space, and out into the hallway. I nearly fell down the stairs that led up to the office, a strange feature in this old building. On either side of the stairs up to the office were stairs leading down to the front door. I quickly went down and let Kayla in.

We did a quick walk through of the building and found it intact, untouched, and only slightly dusty. The building was just three floors on top of each other, attached to a large gymnasium and stage. A balcony went around three sides of the gym, and I could see benches for spectators.

"Okay," I said quietly, listening to my echo in the open space. "Let's find a spot to plan." We went over to the corner and I attached a red lens to my flashlight. I didn't want to advertise we were here.

I took out the marker I had swiped from the office supplies and drew a crude outline of the fort and the defenses. "We can't approach from any side, because we'll be seen and the terrain will slow us down. The only option is to go through the front gate, but I don't know how we can get them to open it for us."

Kayla shrugged, and then stuck out her chest. "Maybe I can open it. Men are men, after all."

I shook that suggestion off. "They know you from the ambush you escaped from. They'd be glad to have you back."

Kayla frowned. "Then what are we going to do?"

I slowly shook my head back and forth. "Not sure, but I know we want to hit it tonight, when it's darkest out so their natural defenses are at their lowest." I looked at my watch. "It's seven thirty now, so let's get some sleep and we'll head back out at around one. They should be a lot less vigilant then."

Kayla agreed and we both stretched out to try to get some rest. I knew I wasn't going to sleep, because all I could think about was what Ben had said about Julia. I hoped she was okay, and I wished I had had the courage to tell her how I felt. At least she would have had the assurance that I would be coming for her, no matter what.

I did manage to drift off to sleep, a testament to how tired I had been from the previous days. Kayla was quietly snoring, and a quick look at my watch told me we had another half hour to go. Outside, it was extremely dark, and only a little light from the moon helped to break up the shadows. A small glow came from the north, and I had to assume that was from lights on the fortress.

A movement behind me told me Kayla was up and my suspicion was confirmed when she joined me at the window.

"Did you sleep at all?" She asked, rubbing her eyes.

"A little. It wasn't easy with you snoring," I joked.

"Very funny. I should tell you...what's that?" Kayla looked out the window intently and I followed her gaze. In the slim light, a dark figure was running towards the fortress, but he was using the road on the backside. He stayed to the center of the road, as if he didn't want to bump into anyone or anything, but he moved quickly and silently, as if he had done it a hundred times before. He slipped away into the darkness before I could get a positive look at him, but something in the back of my mind told me I had seen that man before.

"What do you think?" Kayla asked, still looking at the darkness.

"Whoever it was, he's gone now, so we'll just stick to the plan. Let's get moving," I said.

We put back on the gear we had taken off to sleep, and Kayla took the time to put her hair into a tight knot on the back of her head. I didn't blame her. The last thing she needed was for someone or something to grab her hair at the wrong time.

Outside, the night air was cool and still. We crossed the road in silence and made our way back to our observation post under the bushes. I could still see the men at their posts, and it looked like they hadn't moved in the few hours we had gone to sleep. There were lights on the roof of the building that lit up the surrounding area, but only two of them seemed to work, and they were on the side and the back. I thought about slipping over to the darker sides, but something warned me that wasn't a good idea. Ben wasn't stupid, and it would be just like that asshole to have some sort of trap waiting for people like me who wanted to sneak up in him in the dark.

The more I looked at the fortress, the more depressed I got. I couldn't think of a way in that would be quick enough, and Julia and Jake had already been prisoners for several hours. I sat back with Kayla looking at me, and reached a decision. Whatever the cost, I was going to have to try. Hopefully, they would be caught enough off guard that we could take out the majority of them and get inside.

I signaled to Kayla to take the two on the left and I was going to take the two on the right. After that, I was going to pour rifle fire into the two towers and hoped the ricochets would kill the men inside. How I was going to open the gate was still a mystery, but I was running out of options and night.

Just as we raised our rifles and sighted our targets, a voice spoke up behind me.

"I wouldn't do that just yet."

CHAPTER 44

I spun around and tried to see who spoke to me, but there was nothing but darkness. The voice was familiar, but I couldn't place it.

"Who are you?" I whispered. "Show yourself!"

A shadow detached itself from a nearby tree and moved closer. Its smile was kind of lopsided and roguish, like its owner was constantly amused by life. He was armed to the teeth, though, with a rifle, a couple of small satchels, a handgun, and likely a few knives. The handle of what looked like a sword poked out over his shoulder.

The shadow smiled at Kayla. "Hey, baby girl. Your mom's worried about you."

Kayla jumped into the shadow's arms. "Daddy! I'm so glad to see you! I'm so sorry for making you worry, but Ben has Jake and Julia and…"

Uncle Duncan quieted his daughter with a raised hand. "I know, sweetheart. President Jackson called us the minute you left his house. Your Uncle Tommy is around here somewhere. He was sent to do a little scouting and to stir up things a mite."

Something clicked in my mind. "Sent? Who sent him? President Jackson? How did he know about this place?" I asked.

Uncle Duncan smiled. "Actually, one of those guys did." He pointed down the road where two figures were walking up in the darkness. I could barely make them out in the gloom, but as they got closer, I was able to pick out certain things in the darkness. The men were large, one taller than the other, but the shorter one was more massive. They walked with the casual ease of a predator, taking in everything and extremely confident in their ability to handle just about anything. One of the men had a couple of handles sticking out over his shoulders, while the other had a single handle. Both carried rifles, and both were armed with handguns. Each had a knife at his belt and another attached to the strap of the backpacks they were carrying.

When they reached the point where they might be seen by the guards, the two men silently slipped into the brush by the sidewalk and made their way over to where we waited with Uncle Duncan.

As the men approached us, I slung my rifle around to my back and reached out to the taller of the two men. He wrapped me up in a fierce hug, holding me tight for a long moment.

After a minute, he held me at arm's length. "What the hell do you get yourself into this time, Aaron?" He asked.

I shrugged. "Just one mess after another, Dad. Sorry."

My Uncle Charlie stepped up to me. "My daughter is in there?"

I looked at him in the dark, and to tell the truth, I was more than a little intimidated. "She is. I think she's okay, but I don't know. I don't know much," I said.

Uncle Charlie looked at me then looked at my dad. My father nodded and they both stepped out of the brush. I was about to say something about being seen, but then I realized no one was going to see them. All of the guards had vanished, presumably to go to the east side to watch the three houses that had suddenly caught on fire.

My dad stepped out of the shadows and looked over the gate. All I could see was that it was big and impressive. I don't think my father saw it the same way.

"Duncan! I need something to knock on this door with," my dad said.

Uncle Duncan smiled and pulled one of the satchels off of his shoulder. He made some adjustments to the side as he walked over to where my father was standing. Taking the bag by the strap, he swung it hard and flung it over to the gate. It hit the big iron doors and fell to the ground.

"I'd back up, if I was you," he said to my dad as he walked quickly away.

My father and Uncle Charlie stepped to the side of the wall, out of line from the charge. A few seconds later, the night was lit up a second time as the satchel charge blew, blasting the doors apart and sending them sailing backwards. The guard posts by the gate were affected as well, as the explosion ripped into their foundations and sent one of them crashing to the ground. The other was still upright, but the windows were blown away.

The two men didn't waste any time. They rushed to the towers and after checking one guard, they found he was dead. The other guard was still alive, and very much conscious as Uncle Charlie dragged him into the clear.

My dad was very direct with the man. "My name is John Talon. This is Charlie James. This is a really big gun. I want my son and his daughter. Where are they?" My dad was kneeling on the man's chest, holding his old stainless 1911 to the man's sweating forehead. Uncle Charlie had drawn one of his tomahawks, and was staring at the man with such malevolence it was a wonder the man didn't have a heart attack on general principles.

"Th...They're in the l-l-lab. Basement f-f-floor." The guard couldn't keep his eyes off Charlie, who helped the man's fear by smiling evilly.

My dad stood up. "Get lost. I see you, I kill you."

The guard scrambled to his feet and shuffled off into the gloom. When he was near the edge of trees, he shouted out. "Ben's ready for you! He's going to enjoy killing..."

Whatever the man was going to say was lost as he crumpled to the ground. Another figure had stepped out of the darkness and had dropped the man with a brutal smack to the back of his head. I was surprised and relieved when my Uncle Tommy joined the fray.

"Hey, Aaron. Might want to close your mouth before you get bugs in it," he said as he stepped over to us. "Like my distraction, John?"

"Love it. But they're ready for us now. Let's get in. You and Duncan take the high road, Charlie and I will take the low. Aaron, you and Kayla take the middle and get inside. Find Jake and Julia. If it's not one of us, put it down. Clear?"

My dad was all business, but I could see the tension in him. If anything, Uncle Charlie was worse. That man was practically vibrating with energy.

"Go!"

CHAPTER 45

Just one word and the four of them were through the broken gate. Uncle Duncan and Uncle Tommy went through with their guns up, ready to fire at anything that moved. Dad and Uncle Charlie swept through the gate on the left side, separating and drawing their weapons with practiced ease. Kayla and I seemed to stumble along, bringing up the rear, but in truth, we were moving as fast as the others were.

I started towards the building when there was a large metallic crash behind us. I spun around and saw another gate had fallen down, closing off the main entrance. The lights that illuminated the yard and the space around the yard suddenly went dark, forcing our eyes to adjust quickly to the sudden gloom.

A voice came out of the building, somewhere on the second floor, laughing with barely suppressed glee. I thought I was only going to snare the one son, now I have the other and the father as well. And as an added bonus, I have another father and his daughter as well," the disembodied voice cackled. "And what a delight she will be, I assure you!"

My Uncle Charlie said nothing. He just raised his twin tomahawks over his head and beat them together three times. The ringing steel echoed off of the building and sang out over the homes and the canal. He lowered them and stood with them by his sides, his head down as if he was praying.

My father explained this behavior to me once. It was Charlie's way of signaling that this fight was to the end, either his or his enemy's. No quarter would be asked or given, and there would be no holding back whatsoever. Uncle Charlie had just told everyone in that building were dead men.

Ben seemed unaffected, however. In the ensuing silence, he called out. "Allow me to greet you properly, John Talon. Let's see if you're still the killer you were after all these years!"

The piles of debris which made up the walls of the yard weren't really piles of garbage. The flotsam and jetsam of civilization had been attached to hidden walls which swung upward, revealing dark recesses within. Inside those areas, little lights danced and swayed. Only they weren't little lights. They were the glowing eyes of dozens of zombies suddenly freed from their prisons. It was a pretty simple thing to deduce they hadn't been fed in a while. The purpose of the yard was suddenly clear. It wasn't for protection. It was for feeding.

I reacted instinctively, pulling my falchion from its scabbard and preparing to deal with as many zombies as I could. I pulled my tomahawk from its sheath and held it in my left hand. I wanted to be able to kill with both hands swinging.

My father's voice cut through the moans that were coming out of the containers as the zombies shuffled forward, their glowing, unblinking eyes fixated on their targets.

"Aaron! Take the center! Go now!" He yelled.

I understood immediately. He wanted me to get into the building while the group inside might be distracted with the spectacle outside. It would keep them off balance and might gain me some time to find my brother and Julia. He also didn't want to announce what I was doing, either.

Uncle Tommy and Uncle Duncan began firing, and I noticed they concentrated their fire near the building, clearing a path for Kayla and me. I looked back at Kayla and nodded towards the building, and I was relieved to see she understood as well.

CHAPTER 46

We bolted for the glass front of the old school, jumping over dead bodies and gaining the door. I brought the pommel of the sword up and cracked the glass in one blow. Using my boot, I kicked a large picture window in, crashing glass all over the ground. Kayla was right behind me as we went through, and I quickly put away my sword and axe, replacing them with my M1A. I wasn't going to waste time crossing blades with anyone. I was just going to blast them to hell.

The hallways were dark and the only light was coming from the rear of the building where the homes were on fire. I could hear steady firing from the front where my father and uncles were, which was a good thing, since it told me someone was alive and fighting. I needed to make the most of the time I had and find Jake and Julia quickly.

"Where do we go, Aaron?" Kayla asked, working the charging handle on her rifle and chambering a round.

I got my bearings quickly. Since we were in school, there was going to be a few hallways and a lot of rooms. I guessed that the upstairs would be devoted to Ben and his activities. He seemed to have the ego for it. On this floor would be some general living areas and supply rooms. I thought the interrogation rooms and holding cells would be where there would be no chance for escape, which meant downstairs.

"We need to find a way downstairs. If Julia and Jake are here, chances are they're being held somewhere below," I said, walking forward.

"What if Ben took Julia upstairs to his quarters?"

I didn't want to think about that. "Let's get moving and hope we can eliminate possibles." I didn't mention the obvious. That I wanted to eliminate Ben as well.

We moved down the hall, heading south, if my sense of direction was still working. We didn't encounter anyone, and I thought that was fairly odd. I was wired as hell, and if something didn't come out and play, I was going to start shooting just for giggles.

At the end of the hall, the route took a sharp left turn, and I walked wide, crouching low and trying to be a small of a target as possible. Kayla went to the edge of the corner and when I cleared the outside, she cleared the inside. If anything was unfriendly, it was dead.

That hallway was clear as well, and this was getting downright spooky. Ben went to the trouble of keeping zombies stored for intruders, yet once we were inside, we were free to move around the place? It didn't make sense at all and I said as much to Kayla.

"Something's not right here. There should be guards or traps and what else. These rooms were occupied recently and now they're just empty." I pointed to the room next to me and it was obvious someone had used it for a personal space.

"Well, maybe they're all downstairs," Kayla said. "The nearest stairwell is over there." She pointed to a corner where a set of stairs peeked out at us around a half-closed door.

We crept over and I carefully moved down in the dark. I didn't want to use my flashlight because I had this little phobia about making myself into a target for enemy shooters. At the bottom of the stairs was a set of doors, and a quick check proved they were locked. Likely, there was a crash bar on the other side, but we weren't getting through this way any time soon. I tried to see through the small window, but it was no use. I might as well have kept my eyes closed for all I could see.

"Come on; let's see if there is another way." I led the way back the way we came, moving quickly because I knew it wasn't occupied. That little feature of this place was still strange. We went into an office in the southwest corner of the building, and I risked a small light, cupping my hand over the beam and allowing only a small sliver through. The office looked normal enough, except for one little detail. Every single window had a large desk pushed in front of it. At first, I thought the people here just wanted to see out, but then I realized it was intended to keep things from getting too far if they broke in.

"What's that?" Kayla asked, pointing to an area in the next office.

I looked closely. "Might be what we're looking for," I said.

We stepped over to the small bit of metal railing that was sticking out of the middle of the floor in the central office. I turned the light down to see a circular stairway leading into a very black hole.

"Guess we found our way down. Wonder why they have a stairway here?" Kayla asked.

"Probably to save time from running down the hall. These old buildings have all kinds of shortcuts and passageways. Lets' go," I said. "Maybe anyone down there will think we're supposed to be here and not shoot us in the legs."

"Christ, Aaron, did you have to say that?"

I moved as fast as I could down the stairs, letting the full beam of my light find the stair and area below. When I reached the bottom, I stopped suddenly. I let my light shine around slowly and it revealed about a dozen men lying on the floor. Most of them had been either stabbed or slashed to death. Throats had been cut, chests had been stabbed, and arteries had been severed. I began to suspect I knew where all the men had gone and why we hadn't met with any resistance. Question was, what could have brought them all down here? This wasn't a zombie attack; this was something else.

CHAPTER 47

Kayla came down quickly and stopped as suddenly as I had. Her light was on and added to the lit area. She moved it around and took in the grim scene.

"My God, what happened here?" She asked. Kayla shined her light through an open door across the slaughter and something seemed to catch her eye. She gingerly made her way to the room and looked inside. "Aaron, there's two more in here. Wait!" She ducked inside and reemerged holding a backpack. "This is Jake's! They must have held him in there! He must have escaped!" Kayla was excited and scared at the same time as she looked at the floor. "Is he here?"

I shrugged and started looking at the bodies. I turned over several, and was relieved each time that I didn't find my brother, but I was getting worried, too. If he had escaped and managed to do this kind of damage, where was Julia? Did something drive him to inhuman rage? Did he see something that threw him over the edge? I was getting a really bad feeling and hoped with all my heart that I was wrong.

I stood up after checking the last man, and he wasn't Jake either. I turned around to find Kayla shining her light down the hallway. From where I stood, I could see a small blood trail on the floor, as if something was bleeding, yet dragging itself along.

Kayla was shaking. In a small voice she said, "Jake?"

I bolted past her into the hallway and saw a small figure huddled into a ball on the floor. His eyes were closed and he was bleeding from a dozen cuts and stab wounds, but he still held a blood-covered knife in his hand. I checked his pulse and by some miracle, I could feel a faint, defiant heartbeat.

"Jake? It's Aaron. I'm here. Kayla's here. You're safe now. Jake, can you hear me? Stay with me, brother." I yanked my backpack off while Kayla cradled Jake's head in her lap. I ripped open the kit, pulling out bandages and antibiotics. I pulled out a water bottle and splashed a little on Jake's face, washing off the blood that was there. Kayla was quietly crying, stroking Jake's forehead and mixing her tears with the water. She held her light to his face, helping me wash him.

Jake opened his eyes slightly and looked up at me, turning a little from the light. "Julia's down the hall. You have to get to her before it's too late. Too late." He closed his eyes again and gritted his teeth in response to a new wave of pain from his wounds.

I was torn in half. My brother needed me, yet he was telling me to go save the woman I loved. I couldn't leave him, yet if I didn't go to Julia, she might die as well. I had to make a decision, because I knew I was losing time. Jake had fought to get to Julia, and he had bought us a way in by keeping the men occupied and dying. She was in obvious danger, so I couldn't make that sacrifice in vain, but I couldn't just run away from Jake.

Footsteps interrupted my thoughts and I swung up my rifle one-handed, ready to blast the life out of anything that came down that hallway. I nearly fainted when I heard a familiar voice call out my name.

"Aaron? You down here? Jesus, what a mess," my father said as he discovered the carnage in the other room.

"Dad! We're here! Jake's hurt bad!" I yelled, putting down my gun.

Footsteps pounded down the hall and my father and Uncle Charlie swept into view. Dad dropped to the ground beside Jake, gathering him into his arms, and gently taking him from Kayla.

My father held Jake and lightly touched his cheek, whispering as he did so. "It's okay, Jake. I'm here. I've got you. Daddy's got you."

I saw Jake's body relax a little when my dad said those words. They triggered a long lost memory of my father coming into our rooms and holding us whenever we had a nightmare or something had scared us. It was such a comfort to know our dad was there and he was ready to deal with whatever was frightening us.

Jake opened his eyes and looked into his father's face. He smiled slightly then said. "Julia's down the hall. Couldn't...couldn't...get to her."

My father looked at Uncle Charlie and me. "We got this, go. Kayla, I need your help, honey."

I didn't wait for Kayla's response. I simply launched myself from the floor with quite possibly one of the deadliest men in the world right behind me. If Julia was in danger or had been hurt, I wasn't sure even bullets would stop her father. All I knew was I sure as hell wasn't going to get in his way.

CHAPTER 48

We ran down the hall and stopped by a steel door. I didn't wait for anything. I just yanked the thing open and went inside. About halfway through the door I realized I had forgotten my rifle back by father and brother. As a precaution I pulled my tomahawk stepped into a nightmare.

I stopped about three steps into the room and it took a moment for my mind to adjust to the horror I saw all around me. There was a dim fluorescent light flickering intermittently overhead, and its pale light actually made things worse. I heard a sharp intake of breath behind me and I knew Uncle Charlie was seeing the same thing I was.

The room was large, about forty feet long and thirty feet wide. Arranged in rows were about twenty reclining chairs. In each chair was a young woman, ranging in age from fifteen to thirty. Their hands and feet were secured to the chairs, and their heads were secured to the headrests by leather straps. Each of them had a second leather strap that held their jaws closed, with a third going across their mouths.

Every single one looked at us, and each of them hummed a groan through their gags. All of them were zombies.

As I slowly walked forward, the horror intensified. Every captive zombie had a thin tube attached to the back of their necks, and those tubes were filled with a dark liquid which gathered in a small vial hanging off the back of the chair.

I finally understood where the zombie fluid we had been fighting came from. I looked around frantically, trying to identify Julia in the dim light, but it was difficult, since several of the women were young and blonde, and the leather straps obscured their features. Uncle Charlie went to the other side of the room, trying to find his daughter.

Both of us froze as a door on the opposite side of the room opened and a short man wearing glasses walked in. He didn't notice the two of us at all. He just went over to a woman in the corner who struggled and was staring at him with big blue eyes.

As he approached her, the man pulled out a syringe from his coat pocket. I couldn't see it very well, but I could tell it had something very dark in it. It didn't take three guesses to figure out what it was. The man spoke as he walked.

"Well, I'm sorry it has to be this way, young lady. But Ben says he wants you converted for your reunion with your father, and that's that. Too bad, though. I would have liked to have taken a turn..."

Whatever the man was going to say was lost to the world as two tomahawks slammed into his head. Mine took him by the temple and Uncle Charlie's took him right behind the ear. The impact of the two axes was strong enough to knock the man off his feet and into the wall next to him. The syringe he was holding ironically wound up impaling his leg.

I ran over to the captive and with quick jerks of my knife, freed Julia from her bonds. She burst out of the chair and wrapped herself around me, alternatively kissing me and hugging me. I returned the favor with near desperation.

This went on for a minute until a grunt behind me made me realize who was still with me. I pulled Julia off me and turned around, facing my Uncle Charlie who stood with a second tomahawk in his hand.

"*Daddy!*" Julia burst out, grabbing her father around the waist and burying her face deeply in his chest.

Uncle Charlie just held his daughter for a long moment, breathing her in, wrapping his huge arms around her, protecting her. I felt a little awkward so I concerned myself with pulling the axes out of the head of the man we had killed.

Julia smiled up at her father and asked very seriously, "Where the fuck have you been?"

I nearly laughed at the look on Uncle Charlie's face, but then I realized I kind of wanted to know that as well. Julia stepped back, wrapped her arms around my waist, and looked up at me, not waiting for her father to reply.

"Did you find Jake?" She asked. "He was being held in a cell down the hall."

Oh, shit. Jake. "Come on!" I said, giving the second tomahawk back to its owner as I raced past the secured zombies. There was nothing we could do for these women, but knowing what we knew now, we'd definitely be back to send them over the divide for the final time.

CHAPTER 49

We rounded the corner to see my father hovering over Jake. He had taken Jake's shirt off and was cleaning his wounds, using my first aid kit. Jake was wincing and breathing heavily, his head cradled again in Kayla's lap.

Uncle Charlie went over to my dad and tapped him on the shoulder. Dad looked up and got out of Charlie's way. Julia ran to Kayla and put her hand on her shoulder, her other hand covering her mouth.

Kayla looked up and smiled briefly at Julia. "He was fighting to get to you. He took out a dozen men to try to get to you."

Julia knelt by Kayla and put her hand on Jake's forehead. I felt like a fifth wheel with nothing to do. Charlie worked over Jake, patching his wounds and probing for anything that might be life threatening. After about ten minutes, there was a noise at the top of the stairs, and then two sets of feet came lumbering down the stairs.

I nudged my Dad, who looked up quickly, then kept his gaze on his son.

Dad said softly, "Wait for it."

In the dark, I heard two sets of, "Holy shit."

My dad smiled to himself briefly, and then his face turned serious again. Charlie checked Jake up and down, and then looked up.

"If we can get him to the capital, then he has a pretty good chance. We can move him, but nothing too crazy. Who's going?"

Kayla spoke up first. "I am." Her father looked at her curiously, but wisely said nothing.

Jake suddenly opened his eyes and looked up at Kayla. "Love you, too," he said softly before closing his eyes again.

Kayla started to cry and rocked Jake's head softly, kissing him gently on his bruised forehead.

Julia spoke up. "I'll see him there. We should be okay." She looked over at me expectantly, and I didn't disappoint.

"That goes for me, too, by the way," I said, causing Julia to blush and her father to scowl.

"Talon's are all the damn same," Charlie growled. "You and I have a few things to discuss." He directed that at me and strangely, I didn't feel any fear.

"When you're ready," I said, mentally cataloguing where my weapons were.

Uncle Tommy spoke up. "Knock it the hell off. We're only patching up one of us today. Ben's escaped, and we need to figure out what to do."

My dad looked up from his son. "What did you find?"

Uncle Duncan found his voice. "You're going to have to see it to believe it."

My dad nodded. "Let's get Jake out of here first. Kayla and Julia will take the boat back; get Jake to the medical center. Then we'll see what there is to see when it comes to Ben."

We gathered our gear, and my dad and Charlie gently picked Jake up off the floor. They carefully brought him up the stairs, and then my dad took Jake and carried him all the way back down to the canal. I have to say I was impressed. Mid-fifties and still strong as an ox. My good humor was tempered by the fact that my father's best friend, and person who my father had always described as being stronger than he was, the father of the woman I was sleeping with. If we finished this, I figured I was dead.

At the boat, my dad gave Kayla and Julia instructions and sent them on their way. Julia gave me lingering kiss and mouthed, 'Love you' at me. I swear I could feel my Uncle Charlie's stare on my back.

"Let's get this done," my dad said as he watched the boat move away. Part of me wondered why he wasn't going with, but I realized there was nothing he could do. He knew Jake was going to be in as good of hands as he could find, and if he had lived this long, he was going to make it.

CHAPTER 50

We went back to the fortress, and in the early light of the morning, I could make out the dozens of corpses liberally sprinkled all over the front lawn. Most of them died with headshots, but there were a few with some serious head trauma. A few were close to the front door, and I realized how near we had been to a nasty situation in the school.

Uncle Tommy led the way. "We went up top, figuring on killing Ben and his men. We got the last few of his men, but you have to hand it to the bastard." Tommy made his way to a side stairwell, and passed through the double doors. He flicked on a light and showed us the body lying there. It was a living man, or was, and he had been stabbed with something long and pointy. I suspected said something was resting on my Uncle Duncan's back.

Passing through the doors on the top floor, I was surprised at how clean and neat everything was. There wasn't a scrap of paper, a rag or anything out of place. Looking into the rooms, they were empty of absolutely everything. In a way, it was kind of creepy and weird.

"Down here," Tommy said. At the back of the building was Ben's apartment, apparently. It was a large converted classroom with a bathroom, a kitchen, and a huge living area. On one wall was an enormous television, and on the other was a collection of DVD's from before the Upheaval. I had seen a few when I was a kid, but it had been a long time.

My dad looked around briefly, before turning to Tommy and Duncan.

"Empty. What did we need to see?" He sounded slightly agitated as if he was worried about the time we were losing by coming up here.

"Up those stairs," Duncan said.

Behind my dad was a spiral staircase, and this one led upwards. Duncan led the way, and one by one, we joined him on the roof.

Duncan faced us. "We thought we had him when we saw he had run into his apartment, since Tommy could see the whole hallway, and there was no way he was getting out there. When I came in here after him, it was empty, and I couldn't figure out where he went. Then I heard a noise on the roof and found those stairs.

"Up here, I thought I was going to have a showdown, but when I got out in the open, I saw Ben in a small cart flying away to the east." Duncan shook his head. "Wish I had your skill with a rifle, John. I missed the one shot I had at him."

My dad looked off into the distance. "No problem, brother. In this light, I doubt even Logan could make the shot." He walked around the roof for a second. "Off to the east? In a flying cart? That doesn't make sense."

"Yes, it does," I said. I pointed to a small metal tower bolted to the back end of a brick wall. "There's a cable up there. Who wants to bet our friend Ben went down a zip line?"

"Son of a bitch," Charlie said. "Where does it go?"

"One way to find out," Duncan said. He grabbed a metal bar from a pile of debris, put it on the wire, and held on with both hands. Without another word, he started sliding away.

"Duncan! You idiot!" Uncle Tommy yelled. "You don't know where he went!"

In the darkness, a voice drifted back. "Knowing Ben, it wasn't dangerous!"

We all nodded at the truth of that statement and we went looking for our own zip line bars. My dad and Charlie found a length of rebar that would work, while Tommy happened on a piece of wood. I wasn't having any luck until my foot hit a length of cable obviously left over from the line's construction. That should do.

Tommy went after Duncan, and I followed a little bit later. I have to admit I was sweating about stepping off a roof into the darkness, but nothing bad seemed to happen to the two guys ahead of me, so off I went.

The descent was fast but not crazy, and I had to hold down the urge to shout out. It was actually a lot of fun, sailing over the trees and homes, then sliding between the trees and homes, until I finally reached the end of the line. There wasn't any sudden stop. It was just a descent until I could touch the ground. I almost tripped when I landed, but caught myself just in time.

My uncles were waiting for me and one held up seven fingers and the other eight.

I looked at them curiously and Uncle Duncan said I needed to stick the landing, whatever the hell that meant.

A noise behind me meant my father and Charlie were on their way, and a few seconds later, they joined us at the base of the zip line.

"Where are we?" Tommy asked, looking around for signs.

"Train station," my dad said. "This is the Metra line for Blue Island."

"Where does it go?" Charlie wanted to know.

"South it goes to University Park. North, it goes to the city," Dad said.

"Which way did Ben go?" I asked.

"Let's find out."

We ran up the stairs and out onto the platform. We were just in time to see a small electric rail car disappearing into the horizon. There wasn't any doubt as to who might be in it.

Charlie swore. "Why the fuck would he go north?"

My Dad shook his head. "It figures with what Jackson talked about. He was afraid something like this might have happened."

"What's that?" I asked.

"Ben has set up his real shop in the city. It's perfect, in a way. Surrounded by millions of zombies, he's left virtually alone to live, kill, and create as he pleases. If he's found a safe place, he might never come out," my dad said.

Uncle Tommy groaned. "I guess I know what this means."

My dad nodded. "Yep. We're going to Chicago."

CHAPTER 51

"He knows we're following."

"Maybe."

"Maybe. There's going to be traps and shit if he thinks we're behind him."

"Yep."

"He's not going to just lie down and die."

"Nope."

There was a brief pause. "Good."

I listened to this exchange between my father and my Uncle Charlie as we rolled down the railway line. Ben had made his escape on a strange little contraption that allowed him to ride a small scooter on a single rail. That much we had seen. We spent the next twenty minutes figuring a way to follow. What we had come up with was crude, but simple. We had commandeered one of the small repair vehicles that once upon a time had worked in the rail yards. However, this one was long since dead. So we made do by taking turns, pushing the thing while the others rode.

At first, it was difficult to push, but once we got it rolling, it wasn't hard at all to keep it going. Currently, I was awaiting my turn, when my dad swung around the small tower in my direction. I waited for him to sit down and to get settled before I let loose what had been on my mind for a long time.

"Why'd you leave us?" I said, looking him in the eye.

My dad's eyes narrowed, and for a second I thought he wasn't going to answer. But his eyes cleared and he looked away before answering.

"After your mother died I was just lost. We'd been through so much together, surviving the Upheaval, fighting the Zombie War, rebuilding the country. At least, most of it, anyway. I never thought after all that she'd go out from a disease that *wasn't* the Enillo Virus." Dad cleared his throat. "When she and Rebecca were buried, Charlie and I just couldn't face that lodge. You, Jake and Julia were off doing your own thing, so you clearly didn't need us for anything. So one day, we just put our gear on and wandered off."

Dad smiled. "Funny thing is, we thought you'd come after us and we'd have gone home with you. But you never did, so we just kept moving."

I frowned in protest. "Your note said not to follow! What did you expect?"

"I actually figured you'd have listened as well as you had before, which was not at all. But maybe it all worked out for the best." Dad gave me a wry smile. "You seemed to know what to do when the events required it." He put a hand on my shoulder. "I'm proud of the way you and Jake handled yourselves. You're as good as Charlie and I ever were, maybe even better."

"I don't know about that. And these days, Uncle Charlie seems like he wants to rip my heart out," I said.

Dad grinned. "Don't be foolish. You can deal with him. Besides, he knows if he hurts you, his daughter will probably kill him. Speaking of that, by the way, what's the nature of this new territory between you and Julia?"

Right away, I felt uncomfortable. I wasn't sure what I should say to my dad, and whether or not he really wanted to hear it. In the end, I just decided on the truth.

"I love her, Dad. When I'm not with her, I worry about what she's doing and whether or not she's safe. I want to hide her away, but at the same time, I want to show her off and let the world know she's mine." I looked down. "I know it sounds stupid, but..."

Dad laughed out loud. "Well done, boy. Sounds like the real thing. Just do one thing and you'll be all right."

"What's that?"

"Make her the center of your life. Always think of her, and always keep her close. Sometimes, that will make you miserable, but most of the time, it's the best way to get the most out of life as we have it," Dad said.

"Is that how you felt about Mom?" I asked.

My father looked down. "I've had the good fortune to have been loved completely by two good women. Most men have trouble finding one." He looked up again at me. "You'd better keep yours, and don't do anything foolish."

I looked at the rails. "Like chasing a ghost into the middle of a city infested with decades-old zombies?"

Dad grunted in laughter. "Yeah, that."

I smiled and realized it was going to be my turn at the rails soon. I worked my way to the back and watched briefly as my Uncle Charlie lay at the rear and pushed with his powerful legs. The rear of the vehicle had a platform which allowed us to lie down, dangle our legs over the side, and then push at the contraption. It seemed too good to be workable, but surprise of surprises, we were actually moving along at a good clip.

I thought about what we were going to do and what needed to be done afterwards. I never considered that we might fail, that we might die. That never entered my thinking. Right at the moment, I gave some considerable thought to the situation and about where we might be going.

"Hey, Dad?" I started. I had an idea, but I wanted to see whether it was sound.

"What's up, Aaron?" My father put down his sharpening stone and his tomahawk.

"Where would Ben go, in the city?"

My father shrugged. "Could be anywhere, I guess. Any building, any place."

"Where does this line go?"

My dad thought about that one. "I think, if memory serves me correctly, that this line goes all the way to LaSalle Street."

I thought for a minute. "Is that the one that runs about the middle of Grant Park?"

My dad was taken slightly aback. "How the hell do you know about Grant Park?"

It was my turn to shrug. "I've made about fifteen runs into the city as a Collector. I've studied more maps on the damn place than I can count."

"No shit. Well, you might be of use after all. Any ideas where Ben is, smarty-pants?" My dad looked at me with what might have been new respect.

I grinned. "Just one, but he'll have to make the right moves to prove it."

CHAPTER 52

I left my perch and went to the back to relieve Uncle Charlie. He looked at me, but didn't say anything. I figured my dad would set him straight soon enough, if anyone would. I lay down on the platform and got the swing of things with my legs. I just pushed along, keeping the pace. It wasn't so hard when the tracks stayed level and smooth. It took us a bit to get it going, but after that, it was pretty simple. Stopping it was going to be interesting, since it was about three tons of steel rolling along, but we'd probably be off it by then, anyway.

An hour later, we were rolling through the outskirts of the city. Thanks to the efforts of the Metra system in times past, the railway was protected by chain-link fences on both sides, which in turn protected us. There were gaps and occasionally we passed a surprised zombie, but none of my uncles shot them as a matter of habit.

After a few minutes, I began to feel a shift in the landscape. It was getting a little easier to push the cart, and we seemed to be going faster. That was when I realized we were going downhill, preparing to go underground to where the station was.

I stopped pushing for a second and saw we were still moving, and even going a little faster. I climbed up to join the others and saw that we were indeed about to go underground.

"Any sign of Ben?" I asked.

Uncle Tommy shook his head. "Haven't seen anything new, so he has to still be ahead of us."

"Think he'll try an ambush?" Uncle Duncan asked.

"No," I said. "He's alone and in a hurry. He'll get to his safe place and wait for us to try to get him. That is, if he thinks we're following him."

Four surprised faces looked at me in the early morning light. My father spoke first.

"Explain your thought, son," he said kindly.

"Ben left the building before Uncle Tommy and Uncle Duncan was even close. He bailed on his men long before the fight was over. He took a standard route out of the suburbs and straight to his fortress in the city. He has to figure we'll just take our wounded and go, and he can decide on his next move," I said.

Uncle Charlie spoke up. "Sounds reasonable. We haven't seen him or given any sign he's seen us. How far ahead do you think, Aaron?"

"I figure a good two hours. It's a safe bet his method of transportation is a little more sophisticated and faster than ours on the railway," I said. "Speaking of which, we're about to crash into a train." I pointed ahead of us and grabbed my pack.

CHAPTER 53

There were shouts of 'Whoa!' and general confusion as we scrambled to get off our ride. The big vehicle lumbered along, and a few seconds later, slammed into the back end of a small modified rail car. The very loud bang was amplified by the cavernous station we were in, and I only hoped that wasn't like ringing a dinner gong to the nearest zombies.

Uncle Charlie took the lead. "Let's get out of here. There's bound to be some exploration about this noise."

"Right," my dad said. He took out his pickaxe. "We're in serious shit here. No shots unless we have to. I'd rather not have two million zombies up my ass."

My other two uncles took their melee weapons out and slung their rifles over their shoulders. I took the hint and did the same, pulling out my falchion and looking the blade over. Duncan smiled and Charlie raised an eyebrow at me, but nothing was said. I knew I was going to have to show what I could do to be part of this team, and I was okay with that. For the amount of time I'd been in this city, this was more my territory than theirs.

We went into the gloom of the train station, and I jumped a mite when I felt a nudge on my shoulder. Uncle Duncan smiled and pointed to a reception area just inside the main boarding platform. There were several skeletons and bones scattered throughout the seats and vending machines, but Duncan was pointing to the fact that all of the corpses were seated, either on a chair or on the ground. It was one of the creepiest things I had seen in a while.

After a small inspection, we found that the exits to the street had been sealed off, and the underground passageways to other stations were shut off as well. The only way out was the way we had come.

My dad spoke first. "We missed something. Ben had to come this way; there wasn't any way to get off the track. Split up, use your radio, find out where he went."

I decided to go back to the track and do some scouting. Ben's vehicle was there, and it was an interesting contraption. About thirty car batteries had been attached to a small railcar frame there was a small cab for a single passenger. The controls simply read forward and reverse. An electric powered engine moved the wheels, and with a small push, the cart moved along. There were two fans attached to the platform, and with the wires sticking out of them, I saw they were attached to a generator for replenishing the batteries. Pretty efficient.

I looked at the ground and saw a faint pathway in the stones of the rail yard. Creatures of habit used the same easy trails over and over, and humans were no different than animals in that respect. I pulled out my flashlight and held it low to the ground, extending the beam along the stones. The pathway showed up as a shadow that led across the yard towards the far platform.

That was interesting. Ben seemed not to have gone into the station at all, but instead headed towards the side of the platforms. I walked in that direction, and climbed the short ramp to the platform. There was a lot of debris around here, but no trains, other than the one we had run into, belonging to Ben. Some attempts by nature to reclaim the area were obvious, but those were futile. The sun didn't hit this area for much past the early morning and early evening, and even then, it was slight. A mess of weeds was over on this side, and I could see that there had been recent passage by the broken stems down by the base of the plants.

I walked on the platform, shining my light down and around. There were footprints moving back and forth to a small utility door tucked away in the corner of the platform. It was hidden from the main lobby and waiting area by a small office. I opened the door slightly and looked around. The windows of the office were broken and furniture was thrown around, like there had been a struggle. No surprise there, this town was full of struggles and broken windows.

I looked over the door and there was a small handle down near the middle of it. Just a foot below normal, and easily missed. *Not bad, Ben, not bad at all. Not good enough, though.*

I felt a hand on my right shoulder and I turned slightly to see which uncle of mine it was. Unfortunately, it was Uncle Zombie, and he didn't look like he was happy to see me.

"Jesus!" I said, ducking down and spinning away from the snapping teeth that aimed for my neck. I dove forward and rolled on my left shoulder, coming up out of my crouch with my sword up as the grey skinned, glowing eyed monster snarled at me and advanced in my direction. His skin was hanging off in decaying strips about his face, and his clothing looked like it had been meant for a much bigger man. His nose had decayed away, giving his looks a vicious appearance. His hands reached for me again and his eyes glowed with malice.

I didn't waste time with anything fancy. I just used the point of the sword and speared the ghoul through the left eye. I kicked him off my sword and swung the blade back, flinging black zombie brains out over the yard. I wiped the blade off and looked around, checking for other threats. I didn't see any, other than my Uncle Charlie who looked at me for a second, then at the zombie. He nodded his head slowly and I felt a lot better, as if I had passed a test or something.

My dad walked into the yard a second later and saw me with a dead zombie. He came over, followed by Charlie. Both of them looked puzzled.

"What do you have, Aaron?" My father asked.

"Chasing a rumor," I said. "I went back to the cart Ben used and saw he had been there before and had worn a small trail. The tracks led to this door, which I would figure leads up to the streets."

My dad nodded. "Did you try the door?"

"Not yet, I was interrupted," I replied. "But here goes." I pulled on the latch as Tommy and Duncan walked in. They shook their heads at my dad, who nodded.

The door swung open silently, and I stepped back as my father and Charlie swept up the stairs. They were gone for a minute, and then they were back. My dad came through first, and he didn't look happy.

"What's up? We heading after him?" Duncan asked.

My dad shook his head. "We got to the street, and there was a passage to a ladder to the elevated tracks. But the way was padlocked and we can't get it off without causing a ruckus."

"Would that be a problem?" Tommy asked.

"Only with the thousand zombies I saw up there," Uncle Charlie said.

"That bad?" Uncle Duncan asked.

"That was just on the left," Charlie answered.

"I need options. Aaron, you figured you knew where he was going. Now's the time for a strategy." My dad looked at me as he spoke, and I knew that tone of voice. Whatever he wanted, he wanted it *now.*

CHAPTER 54

I looked at the four men in front of me. I had known these men all my life and had heard countless stories of their bravery, lunacy, and determination. I felt a little intimidated by the experience before me, but I pressed on, confident in what I had to say.

"I think I know where Ben went," I said. "Given the territory, and the lengths he's gone through to establish a base of operations, I'd say he's at Navy Pier."

All of the men nodded, and Uncle Duncan winked at me, which encouraged me to go on.

"It makes the most sense. The high-rises are good, but there's no escape route. The Pier has water on three sides and an easily defended entrance. If he's blocked off one of the sides, it's even easier. He'd have the entire place to himself, a supply of water and food, and sustainable power with solar and wind," I said.

Charlie looked at my dad. "Why the hell didn't we come here instead of the lodge?"

My dad arched an eyebrow at his friend. "When you finish counting the zombies in the city, you'll have your answer," he said.

"Anyway," I continued. "It makes sense that he went to the elevated tracks, and chances are pretty good there's another one of those carts up there. The tracks go to the street just in front of the Pier, so it's an easy commute. He could come and go all day, and no one could touch him."

"How do we get there without getting chased by a million Z's?" Duncan asked.

"We'll have to fight a bit, but follow me," I said, turning around and walking to the opening of rail yard. I swung my sword a bit to loosen up my shoulders and loosened my tomahawk. I adjusted the strap on my rifle and moved it to a more comfortable position. Behind me, I heard my dad chuckle and my Uncle Charlie say, "Good Lord, is he your son!"

I knew once we reached the outside of the yard we'd be more or less in line with the streets. It was a good bit of a hike, but I stayed focused, looking out for the occasional zombie that might have gotten through the fence and wandered this way. As it was, I expected our little crash when we got here to have stirred things up a bit. I knew when we reached the streets we were going to stir them up something fierce. If Charlie thought he saw around a thousand zombies, then he probably did. Uncle Charlie was good for understatement, not exaggeration.

As we approached the big opening, I started to step wide to look around the corner. I had been nearly caught before by lurking ghouls, and didn't feel the need to repeat that mistake. The caution was rewarded, as a small zombie was bumping around the debris piled around the corner. There was a pile of tracks, a bunch of barrels, and some railroad ties that were loosely stacked. The zombie, a female by the color of her clothes, saw us as we stepped into the light. She hissed loudly and lumbered our way, reaching for the first person she saw.

It was her bad luck that she chose my father. I had seen him kill zombies before, and this was no different. He simply waited with the pick on his shoulder for the former woman to get close, and then he pounded her head with his pickaxe. She fell like her strings had been cut, and he held the end of the pick handle as she fell down. A quick kick with his foot released the pick and a stroke and a twist cleaned it off. During the whole encounter, he never even used both hands.

"Come on, we've got to move," I said. "If we can get ourselves down the street and to the river before too many of them know we're here, then we've got a chance."

"So we're depending on luck, are we?" Duncan asked with a smile, taking a two handed grip on his sword.

"Jesus, we're screwed," said Tommy, rolling his neck and cracking his knuckles.

"Just lead the way, Aaron, we're right behind you," Dad said. "If we can't keep up, just keep going. Do not stop for us. This bullshit with Ben ends today."

"Just move," I said, stepping quickly into the light and letting my eyes adjust. I scanned the skyline quickly, looking for a quick way to get to the river. I knew I wanted to go west and I knew it was pretty close, but I hadn't been to this part of the city before and there might be obstructions I didn't know about. Couldn't be helped. Right now, I had to believe we had the element of surprise, and we had to use it fully. Ben had been calling the shots for a while now and it was time to shut him down.

I looked at the fence by the yard and decided it wasn't worth getting tangled up in. Besides, there was a bridge a little further down that didn't have any fence, so I decided to take the path of least resistance. Twenty yards down the rails and I was looking over a viaduct that had about fifteen cars jammed in it, and at least two trucks. Three zombies that were standing in a shadow slowly extricated themselves and starting moving in our direction. In about fifteen seconds, they were going to be directly beneath us.

"Here goes," I said, jumping off the bridge onto the roof of the truck. I tried to land as lightly as I could, but it seemed to be enormously loud under the rails. Deep in the dark tunnel, I could see several shapes moving about as they shuffled forward to see what the ruckus was all about. I knew it was just the start and it was going to get worse before it got better.

I squatted down and jumped to the roof of the car, sliding a little on the dusty surface. I corrected and stepped off, directly in front of the three zombies. I slipped my tomahawk out of its sheath and hurled it at the nearest one, splitting his skull and dropping him. One of the nice things about the original ghouls is they were in a serious state of decay. The virus preserved them only so long, and then time and the elements worked on them to the point where they were nearly fragile. Nevertheless, they were still lethal of you weren't paying attention.

As the one fell, I jumped over his body and swung my sword with both hands, severing the head of the left zombie. She was an old woman, who was missing half her torso, but her other half was still wearing a flowered robe. The last zombie lurched forward and I hit him in the head with a backhand swing that took the top third of his head off. I pulled out my tomahawk and wiped it quickly.

I looked for threats and saw plenty, but I was more concerned with the rest of the crew getting down off the bridge. I moved into the shadows of the tunnel, trying to keep between them and the advancing, eyeball-glowing darkness.

I was just about to start swinging when a fourth set of boots landed on the car and jumped off.

"Let's go, we're good," my dad said, coming up behind me to help if needed.

"Right. I got point," I said, spinning around and running from the zombies, my dad right on my heels. We passed the three corpses and I thought I heard one of my uncles say out loud that he was glad I was on his side. Not sure which one, though.

CHAPTER 55

I took off to the north because there was a big damn building to the west. We ran between two tall buildings, and crossed a very crowded street. There were cars everywhere, and we had to be very careful around the trucks. Duncan would drop quickly, check for feet, and then yell 'Clear!' as needed. When there was a killing to be done, then either I took care of it or one of the others did. It was fascinating to watch them work together. No one talked, they just knew what everyone was going to do and they just did it.

I hoped we were going to be able to make it to the river without too much trouble, but as we made our way through the trucks, cars, burned out vehicles and junk all over the street, we were slowed down enough that the zombies hiding out in the buildings and alleyways were becoming aware of our presence. It didn't help at all to have a few of the more vocal ones let loose in the canyons of the city, moaning loudly enough to warn the ones ahead of us that we were coming.

"Dammit," I said as I looked over the cars and advancing zombies.

"What's the trouble, son?" My dad said as he walked up to my side.

"Well, we need to be there, and they're there, and it's a headache from here," I said, making sense to no one in particular.

"Backtrack?" He said, looking back the way we came.

"Side road, but we're going to have to be quick. Come on," I said, going back the way we came. I figured we could take the short route south and be able to deal with a smaller road than this wide one we were on. All we were doing was asking for trouble, and it was coming at us from both directions. I ran back the way we came and saw a good-sized horde bearing down on us from the east. Add to the zombies coming from the west we were right in between seriously screwed and royally boned.

I raced past Tommy and Duncan, who started running with me and ran straight at the zombies coming from under the tunnel. When I was barely ten feet from them, I veered south, heading down a very narrow street. The buildings were tall on either side, and the whole corridor was darkened from lack of sunlight. Weeds and debris lined both sides of the street, and a number of very dark places were there that likely held very dark things. The light at the end of the tunnel was that we would be able to limit who came after us if need be, but I was hoping it wouldn't come to that. I was also worried about the ones who might be in the stores and shops, waiting for a meal to walk by.

I moved down the street and stole a look behind me. All four of the men were keeping up easily, watching the corner and shadows, careful where they put their feet as we moved past the buildings.

"Look out!" Duncan called, bringing his weapon up. Three zombies came stumbling out of the ruins of a fast food restaurant. They looked grey to black in color, and their eyes were nearly white from the disease. What was left of their clothes was full of holes, dirt, and dried blood. The lead zombie, a tall man with holes rotting his face, stepped out at a rather quick pace towards Duncan.

Duncan ducked under the zombie's outstretched arms and got behind it. Thrusting his sword almost backwards over his shoulder, Duncan speared the dead thing through the back of the head. Not waiting for the ghoul to fall, he wrenched the blade out and used the momentum to cut a wide swing at the other two. The razor edge of his sword easily cut the heads off the two remaining zombies, and Duncan used the tip again to end the snapping of the still animated zombie heads.

"Clear," Duncan said, wiping his blade off quickly.

"Keep moving," Dad said. "You got a plan at the end of this road, Aaron?"

"Yes, sir," I said, moving on. "But we can't get there from here if we stay still."

We stepped ahead and I circled wide around a couple of cars that looked like something might still be in them. Behind us, the zombies swayed and pursued, lurched and chased. They were seeing a meal for the first time in years, and the hunger must have been insane.

Ahead of us, two trucks were smashed together and blocked the whole street. Cars on either side blocked the sidewalk, and the decay of two decades filled in the gaps.

I looked over the situation quickly, trying to figure a way around. We couldn't go back, and forward was delayed. We couldn't even go under the trucks without being blocked, as there were cars on the other side that had rusted to the ground.

Looking at the truck again, I got an idea. I sheathed my sword and ran to the back of the truck on the left. It was a long box truck, with a lift on the back. The back end was jammed tightly against the side of a building, and I wasn't going that way. However, since around and under was blocked, and through wasn't an option, I decided on up. Stepping up on the back bumper, I put my foot up on the side rail and pushed up, reaching to grab the roof of the truck. One hand made it and I used the momentum of my legs to roll the rest of myself onto the roof. It was dirty, dusty, and covered in filth, but it was empty and looked great to me.

I stood up and gestured to my family. "Get over here, I'll hoist you up. Dad, give me your pickaxe."

My father understood immediately and handed up his axe. I reversed the weapon and held the handle while they grabbed the metal. I pulled up Duncan and Tommy, and then pulled up Charlie. I think he expected me to struggle with him, but in truth, he was lighter than I expected. My dad came up last, and it was a near thing with the horde of zombies right on his heels. The moaning they started bounced off the narrow walls of the buildings and echoed out towards the open lands.

On top of the truck, we looked out over the barricade. In front of us was a sea of cars, stretching south as far as we cared to see. The cars were rusted hulks, with the glass long smashed away and weird things growing inside them. Several had given way to the elements, turning into small mounds of grass and dirt, accumulated from wind and rain. There were even a couple of trees working their way through the old vehicles.

Spaced out all over the place were about a hundred zombies, and even in the few seconds I watched them roam around, another twenty or so joined in from the side streets. Apparently, the word had gotten out about an All You Can Eat buffet.

We were safe where we were, but in a short amount of time, we were going to be trapped with no way to go but to hell.

CHAPTER 56

"If we move fast enough, we can get past most of them," I said. "The way we want to go is right there," I pointed to a space between two buildings and I could see a white building with an interesting curve to the architecture. If I was right, and I was pretty sure I was, then we were a block away from where we wanted to be. Trouble was, that block was going to be a fight.

"Let's rock," said Duncan. "You prefer left or right?"

"Right," I said. "Most of my swings start there."

"So I'm right where they end up? Don't you love your favorite uncle?" Duncan gazed at me with big eyes, which on him looked downright ridiculous.

"I'll take both if you're not up to it," I said, matching his big eyes with my own.

"Will the two of you show-offs just move already?" Tommy said, pointing at the drift in our direction.

"Gone," I said, moving to the front of the truck. I jumped onto the cab, which was a risk, since I could have fallen right through. But it held, and I stepped down to the hood. A single zombie stepped forward to challenge me, and I took the opportunity to jump off, bringing my sword down in a single heavy chop to the top of its head. The razor edge slashed through the head, through the neck, and completely through the torso. I barely managed to stop the swing before I slammed the blade into the ground. The two halves of the zombie fell in opposite directions and I stood up with my gore-encrusted blade dripping onto the ground. As I looked down at my work, Duncan joined me at the front of the truck.

"Cool," he said. "I've always wanted to do that."

"You get the next one," I said. "Let's move before Uncle Tommy yells at us again."

"You get used to it after thirty years."

"Damn. That long?"

"Yup."

We moved down the side street and I was grateful it was only two car lanes wide. There were no stores on the side street, just windows to the stores on the other side. There were a couple of displays that had mannequins in them, and I slowed down to take a look at one of them.

I passed and said to Duncan, "Did that dummy have a bite out of it? Like, around the shoulder?"

Duncan looked back then nodded. "Seen that before. Z's aren't the smartest things around, you know?"

I just kept running, but I had to admit my opinion of zombies just went a notch lower. We burst out of the small roadway into a larger area, and a very interesting building reared up in front of us. It was seven stories tall, and was curved in and out like an 'S' lying down. The building had balconies on all the windows, and they bulged out like white bubbles all over the place. The structure looked like it had been made from really big cauliflower.

"That where we going?" Duncan asked.

"Dead ahead. Follow me," I said. I glanced once to see where the others were and I was glad to find they were right behind me. On the north side of the street, several zombies were coming down the sidewalk, while the south side had a good dozen lurkers that immediately began the undead shuffle. I wasn't going to wait for an audience. I went directly to the building and located the entrance. It was one level above ground, and still in one piece.

I pulled on the handle and was somewhat surprised that it opened. I went inside and approached the second door while Charlie secured the first door with a length of wire.

The inside door was locked, but I had a cure for that. I took my knife out and using the point, jammed it into the metal of the latch that secured the door. A second of twisting and I pulled the door open to let my relatives through.

When we got inside, my dad closed the door and pulled a can of spray paint from his pack. He quickly covered the glass with patterns, swirls and shapes, obscuring the view. When I cocked my head at him, he shrugged.

"Seems to work. If they can't see us, they'll lose interest since they can't smell us either. The paint patterns screw up their sight and they can't make us out," he said.

I'd have to remember that one. However, we had to get through before we attracted any more attention that might alert Ben. For all we knew, he had lookouts stationed on rooftops all over the city. I moved on down the steps towards a large lounge area. There was a lot of papers and furniture about, but no signs of serious violence. It looked more as if people just grabbed what they could and left, hoping for the best. I was hoping they had decided to leave by more conventional means and we would find some much needed transportation help.

"What is this place?" Charlie asked, looking around. There was a bar off to one side, and the remains of a restaurant. A small concierge desk was overturned at one corner, and there was a looted convenience store off to the far side.

"Looks like it was one of those high-end river condo complexes," Tommy said, pointing to the west side. "People would take their boats off the lake and sail them down here for a private mooring."

My dad slapped me on the back. "Goddamn brilliant, Aaron. Let's see if we're really lucky today."

He moved over to the huge glass windows that looked out over the river. The water itself was about twenty or thirty feet below us, and it was impossible to see if anything was still parked at the piers.

CHAPTER 57

"What do you want?"

The voice came from above us and we spun around, whipping our guns up. I didn't have my rifle up, but my pistol was out and ready. My father stepped forward, not lowering his rifle and spoke.

"We need a boat, if you have one. We can buy or trade, your choice." He lowered his rifle slightly, but kept it ready.

Above us, four men with bolt-action rifles looked down from a balcony. A fifth man, a man with blond hair and a lean look to his face, stood off to the side. I thought I had seen him before, and when I stared at him, he seemed to get a little nervous and shifted to put a pillar between us.

"Nothing is for sale or trade. You have no reason to be here, so please leave." The man had an imperious tone that would have been grating in the best of circumstances, and these sure weren't them. I knew my dad was in a hurry because he wanted to get back to Jake, and the fact that he bothered to talk at all to this prick was an exercise in extreme patience.

"We're leaving, and we're taking a boat. We need to settle some business, and then we will return the boat. I'm sure we can work out some kind of arrangement," my dad said, lowering his rifle further.

"I don't deal with your kind. I will tell you one more time, and then the security team will open fire. Your choices are to stay and die, or leave and live," the man said.

Suddenly, I knew I had seen him before. Worse yet, I knew where I had seen him. I needed to make the right move and not get us killed in the process. My dad was about to speak when I signaled him with my hand. I had to holster my gun to do it, but I made it seem like I was trying not to get shot. I held my hand straight down, then held out two, then three fingers.

"All right, we'll get moving. Just tell your men to stand down, okay?" My dad said, lowering his rifle all the way.

"Move now and I'll consider it," the voice said.

"Deal," my dad said. "Go!"

That was the signal. Uncle Charlie and I ran under the balcony on our side and my father, Tommy, and Duncan run underneath on their side. The walkway spanned the entire atrium from one end to the other, and there was a single spiral stairway from the ground floor leading to it. We stayed out of sight under the structure and I used the quick breather to sheath my sword and pull out my heavy rifle.

"Hey! Get out of here or we'll shoot!" One of the security men yelled.

"Don't mind if I do!" I said, bringing up my M1A and firing through the floor. The .30 caliber bullets blew through the metal walkway as if it wasn't there. There were screams, shouts, and a couple of heavy thuds on the walkway.

"Stop! Stop! You'll hit the homes above us! Stop!" The rude man spoke up, much more contrite now that we were in a better position than he was.

"Throw the guns over the side. Now," Tommy said. Four rifles clattered to the ground and he bent over to scoop them up.

Duncan swept up the stairs and there was some snarling, but five men came down the steps. One was limping from a bullet wound in his leg, and another was being helped by third, holding his rear. As he passed by, I saw that one of my bullets had opened up a furrow in his ass cheek.

The blond man stepped in front of my father, and nearly spat his words.

"Fine. Take what you want. Just get the hell out of here. We never wanted your help, and we just want you to leave."

Dad looked him over, and was about to speak when I stepped in. I had put my M1A back and had taken out my sword. Without a word, I rammed the blade through his chest, shoving a foot of steel through his sternum. The man gasped loudly, then pawed weakly at the steel as he slowly fell to the floor. The big blade stuck a little as the man died, and it took a foot in his gut to pull it out.

My dad stared at me with a look I hadn't seen before, and I was sure he was wondering what kind of son I had become. The other men were in shock, and one threw up on the tiled floor. My uncles didn't say anything, they just spread out slightly, and out of the corner of my eye, I could see Duncan slowly raise his rifle to the low ready position.

I looked back at my father. "I met this man before. He was working with the kidnappers at the capital. He was the middleman between the sheriff and Ben. I had seen him before when Julia and I had a run-in with some lowlifes who wanted to take Julia. He probably had a way to get in touch with Ben, and would have told him we were here the second we left."

Charlie spoke up first. "I'm not happy with this, Aaron."

"No?"

"Nope. I wish you had let me kill the son of a bitch."

The tension broke and my dad gave me a half smile that meant more to me than him coming out and saying he was proud of me. It was a look that said he was very glad of how I turned out.

"Your mother would have been proud," he said. "She worried that you would take too long to think about things and hesitate when work needed to be done."

"Wasn't she always saying things like, fools rush in." and all that?" I was a bit confused.

"Yeah, she contradicted herself on a number of occasions. She was who she was, God love her." He shook his head and turned his attention to the four men on their knees in front of us. The men were having a hard time taking their eyes off the body. He squatted down and said seriously, "Now, what do we do with you?"

One of the unwounded men spoke up. "Please don't kill us. We're just security here, taking care of the people who live here."

"How many people?" Dad asked.

"About two hundred."

I was stunned. I had no idea there were that many people alive in this city, let alone in one place. "Why are they here?"

The man shrugged. "There's water, food if you're careful, and we trade with the capital all the time."

"What kind of trade?" Charlie asked.

"Anything we can find. We've been doing well with a few medical buildings and clothing stores," the man said.

I could understand that. There was always a market for clothing and medical supplies were always in high demand. A walker or a wheelchair could cost as much as a full five pieces of silver.

"You ever meet a man about fifty or so, white hair, dead eyes?" I asked casually.

All four men shook their heads. "No one like that has ever been around here. Around fifty? No, sir. Oldest person here is thirty five."

That made no sense. Anyone who stayed here after the Upheaval would be older, and in some cases, considerably. Unless blondie here cleaned house and populated it with friends and kidnap victims.

Suddenly, the light bulb went on. Of course! There wasn't enough zombies at the place in Blue Island to cover the number of people kidnapped, and they had to be kept somewhere they couldn't leave, but nice enough they might not want to leave. Especially if their home back at the capital was a small house or shack.

I waved my dad over. "We need to get out. Let's go while they haven't figured out who we are yet."

Dad nodded. "Agreed. We haven't mucked this up yet, so let's not start now." He turned back to the men. "We're going to use one of your boats. Which one do you use to go on the lake?"

The men looked down, and one answered. "The black one."

"Thanks. We'll bring it back, maybe by this evening," Dad said.

CHAPTER 58

We left the unwounded men tied and gagged, while the wounded men, we treated and locked in an office. It would be a couple of hours before anyone came looking, or was brave enough to investigate the shots, and we would be long gone by then.

The boats were well maintained, and we chose the smallest of the four. It was a bass boat, with a trolling motor and oars. The other boats were too large for our purposes, and would likely raise questions if we showed up unannounced. The biggest one was a large cruiser with black tinted windows. It was easily seventy-five feet long, and would be a very nice boat on the lake. On the canal, though, it would ground itself in a heartbeat past the locks.

We piled into the boat and Duncan pushed us off. If I remembered the river right, we had a little ways to go, follow the water as it flowed to the right, then we'd be making our way across a small harbor to Navy Pier. It was going to get really interesting then.

The trolling motor started right away, and quietly pushed us along the river. Duncan kept us to the shadows cast by the tall buildings, and steered around some debris that looked like it had been there a long time. Under one bridge there was a submerged car.

I used the opportunity to wipe off my weapons and to top off my magazines. My dad watched me for a while, and I knew what was on his mind. But I wanted to wait until he said something.

"You've grown up a lot, Aaron. I have to say that," Dad said. "For a while there, I thought you'd be willing to let us take care of business, but you sure put that fear to rest."

I shrugged. "If you're worried about the man I ran through, don't be. He'd have done the same a hundred times over without batting an eye. He was in league with Ben, and I wouldn't want to guess how many of those girls at the school he was personally responsible for kidnapping. Should I have faced him armed? Maybe. But you were the one who taught me fair fights were for fools."

I could see that Dad was torn a bit inside. One the one hand, I had stabbed an unarmed, surrendered man. On the other, it was a really bad man. In the end, Tommy was the one who broke the dilemma.

"He's dead, and how he got there really doesn't matter, as long as he got there, right? His usefulness was over. If it means anything, Aaron, I'd have shot him, myself, and not cared which side I was facing," Uncle Tommy said.

The rest of the men nodded, and I finally think the matter was at an end. We had more pressing things to worry about. As we travelled, the dead came out to see us by. Hundreds of zombies lined the walkways and the streets, moaning softly as they tracked our progress. One reached out over a rail and fell into the water, disappearing in a swirl of deep green.

We rounded the bend and Duncan slowed the motor, moving as quietly as possible. Charlie, Tommy, my father, and I kept a watchful eye for lookouts and sentries. Our weapons were ready to hand, but not up, keeping our profile as simple as possible.

"What's the layout of this area, Aaron?" Charlie asked quietly.

"The harbor is enclosed, and if we make our way along the north side, we can anchor and get out without being seen," I said. "But the hard part is getting to the Pier itself. It sticks out in the water, so there's no way to approach it without being seen. We'd be under fire the second we pulled out from the harbor."

"What about on land?"

"Odds are better, but we'd have to be really lucky. If there was a way to keep everyone's attention away from the land, then we could make a run for it," I mused.

Dad nodded slowly. "I think we can manage something. We're going to have to get coordinated soon, so listen up."

CHAPTER 59

I moved along the water's edge, trying to keep as low profile as possible. I could see a sentry standing by the front of the entrance to Navy Pier, but I wasn't sure if there was another one. The trees along the water's edge helped a great deal, along with the years of growth from the grass, but they also kept me from seeing things, too. I had no idea if there was a large contingent of zombies making their way over to me or not.

I had slipped out of the bass boat when we made the locks which led to the lake. My father and the crew were going to execute the other part of the plan, which was to distract and attack from another side. If they were very lucky, they would be able to even the odds a little before storming the place.

As I approached, I was hit with a small, nagging doubt. What if Ben wasn't here? What if he had made his way to another destination and we were walking into a major horde of zombies? I began to worry that all the confidence I had felt earlier was wasted. Then I suddenly realized that I could have asked the guy back at the apartments where Ben was, but I killed him before I thought to ask.

"Ah, hell," I said aloud, not thinking about my whereabouts.

I thought about them soon enough as a deep groan answered me from the other side of the trees. That groan was answered by another, and another, and another. I didn't wait for them to come exploring, I kept low and ran for all I was worth, trying to get some distance between me and the spot where they would come looking. Zombies were kind of dumb that way. They zeroed in on a sound and checked it out, and if there was something for them, they killed it.

I ran for about one hundred yards, and then I reached the street. I kept to the overgrown bushes that lined a small, U-shaped turnabout in front of Navy Pier, then without worrying about a sentry, I crossed the road and made my way over to the gate that closed the area off. Ten seconds later, I was inside the gate, hiding behind a small bush, where I tried to catch my breath.

I held my breath, though, when voice above me said very clearly, "What the hell has stirred up Zeke out there?"

Another voice answered. "What are you talking about? They always make noise over here."

The first voice sounded skeptical. "No, this is something different. They got wind of something. Think one of those stupid collectors is sniffing around again?"

"Likely. I'll call it in. Then we'll see if the dumb fuckers want to come over and have their asses saved."

The first voice chuckled. "That was funny. Waving them to the gate then slamming it shut while the zombies are on their tails. Man, they screamed when the zombies started ripping into them. What did that one girl say?"

"'It's not fair! You're not fair!" the first voice said sotto voce, in a mockery of the victims' voice. "She fought pretty good, but they ripped her apart."

"Had nice tits, if I recall correctly."

"Right up to the point where that big zombie bit them off."

"She was still alive when he did that, right?"

"She lived a long time. Her hands were still trying to push them off when they were eating her insides."

I had heard enough. Obviously, I was in the right place. How the hell they didn't see me come over the gate is a damn mystery, but it worked for me. I looked at the wall, and saw there was a window about fifteen feet above me. A large sill underneath it blocked a good part of the view of the gate, which explained why they missed me. A door was further down the wall, and I slipped over to it, trying to keep quiet as I moved through the brush. I didn't know if there were more guard posts, but I began to doubt it. This place was about as secure as you could find in Chicago.

The door opened easily, and I moved up the stairs. What I needed was on the second floor. The corridor I was in was dark, save for a single bulb burning at the top of the stairs. That told me all I needed to know about whether or not this place had power. Given the weakness of the light, there wasn't much, but they had enough for their needs.

I listened at the door for a moment and heard one of the guards talking on the phone. He did a lot of, "Yes, sir." And "No, sir," and finally, I heard, "Okay, sir." I knew then it was time to move. I tuned the knob quickly and quietly, drawing my pistol as I did so. I was carrying a Beretta 92 again, mostly because it was big and carried a lot of bullets.

I opened the door and stepped in, bringing my gun up. Two men were ten feet from me and both had their backs to me. They were three feet apart and one had his feet up on the desk that had been shoved up to the windows. The entire second floor was covered in windows, and by the angle of the man leaning back, he couldn't even see the street, let alone someone under his window. The other man was leaning back now, too, having gotten whatever instructions he was going to get from his superior. I began to wonder how many men were here, but I had to deal with this pair first.

I stepped forward and kicked the legs of the chair of the leaner forward, sending him crashing to the floor. I used my gun like a club and smashed the second man in the teeth as he turned to the noise. The first man I kicked in the head to get his attention, and then kneeled on his chest near his neck. His hands stopped moving towards his waist when I shook my head at him and stuck my gun in his mouth. I pulled a second gun from my waist, my father's stainless old .45. The big gun must have looked huge the man holding his bloody mouth, since his eyes got very large.

I wasted no time. "Cooperate and I won't kill you right away. Don't, and I will. Decide now."

CHAPTER 60

Both men looked at each other and nodded slightly. I got off the man on the floor and put away the 1911. Stepping back, I held the gun on both men as I signaled them to their feet.

"Put those chairs back up. Weapons on the floor. Slowly. Now back up to the window." I gathered the guns and put them in my vest. "Now, who's got the key to the gate outside?" I asked, keeping an eye on both men.

The man I had upended pulled a ring of keys from his belt and held up one. I waved my gun at the stairwell and both men started down. I waited a second to make some space between us, and then followed. At the bottom, I told them to stop.

Pulling some zip ties from my pocket, I told Bloody Mouth to tie his partner's hands together. When he had finished, I did him the same favor. "Wait here," I said.

I slipped outside and checked for any activity. There were several zombies wandering the trees over by the traffic circle, and I could see dozens more in the grassy area just beyond it. That would do. I unlocked the gate and opened it slightly. Hurrying back to the stairwell, I found the men had used their time wisely. One of them was trying to chew through the zip tie of the other, making for a very compromising situation.

I kicked the man doing the biting in the ribs and slammed an elbow into the head of the one getting bit. I was suddenly very mad and the words of the two came back to me about letting that collector die.

"You like to bite things? Then I think you should go where they bite back," I snarled, grabbing the men by their hair and dragging them outside. I didn't give them a chance to shout or raise an alarm; I just threw them outside the gate, shutting it behind them. I gave them a final piece of advice.

"You might have a chance if you run along the water. Maybe." I wasn't feeling very positive about their chances, but then sometimes I just never knew.

The men stood up, looked at their approaching doom, and decided it might be worth it to run. They took off for the lake and disappeared out of sight. The fact that they didn't scream told me several things. One, there weren't that many people here. If there were a sizable force with decent firepower that could have rescued their asses, then they would have stayed and yelled their fool heads off. It also told me that the nearest buildings to the city were likely empty. I wouldn't have much to worry about if I was careful. Lastly, they ran exactly where I wanted them to, which would signal to my father and his crew that I had done my job and the sentries on this end of the pier were taken care of.

That would get us to the next stage of the assault, which was to get everyone to the south side, allowing me to scout and make recommendations for a landing. I thought about going up top to the Ferris wheel, but I had an aversion to being shot out of the sky. Not sure why that bothered me, but it did.

I moved around to the nearest building and checked a door. It was a parking garage, and I was hoping to see plenty from the top side. I didn't bother with the parking area. It would be faster just to take the stairs. I didn't know how long I had before the men I had released were discovered to be missing, but I figured I had an hour at the most.

On top of the garage, I could see most of Navy Pier. It was a massive complex, with restaurants, a shopping center, an amusement park, and a miniature golf place. Along the south side, two huge boats were tied up. One was labeled the Spirit of Chicago, and the other was unknown, the name being hidden. However, the Spirit was enormous, easily one hundred fifty feet long. It looked like it was used for long cruises and for travelling to other states. No way was that big boy going to make it down the river. For one thing, it would never fit under the bridges.

I could see two large buildings toward the far end of the pier, and the furthest had a huge glass dome covering it. I had a feeling about that last place, and was very anxious to try it out. But first things first.

I got out my radio. "Uncle Duncan, you there?"

The response was immediate. "Loud and clear, kiddo. Got your message. Two very scared men just ran past our position, each one looking like he was going to make sure the other guy fed the Z's first. Where are you?"

"I'm on the parking garage, about to head towards the back dome. When are you going to make some noise?"

"Two minutes. Be ready. By the way, your dad wants his gun back." I heard a chuckle from someone in the vicinity of Duncan.

"He can have it. Where's the safety on the dumb thing?" I joked.

"Oh, Lord. Put it away before you shoot yourself."

"Where can he pick it up?" I asked.

"We're on the big boat, so don't worry, we'll get to you."

"Got it. Heading down. Out."

I got back to the ground floor and made my way carefully along the north side. There wasn't much in the way of attractions on this side, so I began to realize I was moving along the service side of the pier, the place where they made deliveries and such once upon a time. It made sense; they sure weren't going to use the lake.

I moved steadily along, and when I glanced back, I saw I had travelled about halfway to my destination. It was then that I heard a huge explosion and even from my side of the Pier I thought I could feel the concussion from the blast. For a brief minute, I wondered if Uncle Duncan had blown up the big boat. A second later, I could see a cloud of dark smoke billowing up into the air. Between the blast and the smoke, I wouldn't doubt if half the zombies in the city were headed this way.

I could hear shouting and it sounded like someone was yelling over a loudspeaker, but they might have been inside a building. I kept to the service road and made my way along the buildings, trying to keep out of sight.

I was crossing another service entrance when a voice behind me shouted out.

"Don't move! Stop where you are and put your hands in the air!"

CHAPTER 61

Damn. So much for surprise. I complied with the order and put my hands about ear-high, turning around slowly. About three feet away from me was a man about my height, although he was a little shorter. He was thin, but looked to have a wiry kind of strength. He had a knife at his belt and a big rifle he was pointing right at my face. That last part was a little disconcerting; I'm not going to lie.

"Who are you? What are you doing here?" The man asked, stepping closer. I could see he was nervous, likely never having to deal with something like this before.

"Don't shoot me, don't shoot me," I said, averting my eyes and ducking my head away. An idea popped into my head and I decided to run with it. "I was collecting in the city and I heard the explosion. All of a sudden, the zombies are all over the place, and I barely made it to the lake before they chased me this way. I climbed the fence and was looking for a place to stay safe until the zombies went home." My words came out in a rush, and I wanted them to be overwhelming.

"All right, all right! Just shut up for a second. I have to take you in, and we'll see what they have to say about you," the sentry said.

"Oh, thanks, man. I got separated from my group and I don't know where they are or even if they're alive. But I'm real glad someone is here to..." I didn't finish my sentence, as I used my little speech to step closer to the man. His gun had stopped pointing at me, and I grabbed it, jerking it away from him, and then shoving it back into his face. His hands came loose and I threw the rifle into the lake.

The man scrambled to his feet. "Son of a bitch! You're gonna regret that," he said, putting himself into what he must have thought was a threatening pose. His hands were up and his feet were apart, obviously expecting me to attack in some preconceived way.

Trouble was, my teachers had one rule when it came to fights and zombies. Win. So without much buildup, I wound up and kicked him in the shin of his foremost leg as hard as I could.

His eyes bulged and he instinctively leaned forward to grab his leg. As he came up, I used the forward motion of his head to increase the impact of the punch I had aimed at his face. His head snapped sideways, and I brought the other fist I had waiting into his collarbone, right below his throat. That punch threw him backward and left him gasping for air on his back. I grabbed him by the ankles and dragged him over to the edge of the pier where I threw him in the water.

I ran from there, trying to put some distance between me and the eventual yelling that would likely erupt form the man in the water. The first person to find him would know I was here, and I wanted to be further away and hidden by that time.

I reached the end of the big building and I was wondering how the heck I was going to get inside, when a small door opened from where the big glass part was and the long brick building. I slid towards the building, trying to seep into the bricks and not get seen. Two men came outside and both were carrying guns. One propped the door open with a small stick.

"Steve's not checked in, think something happened to him?" The first one said, a red headed gent wearing all black. I thought back to the encounter with the all black females up in St Charles and wondered if there was a dress code.

"That dope could drown, for all I care. Damn fool always going on about how he sees things or something's breaking over the barriers. Stupid fuck. Probably thought that exploding propane tank was an attack." The second man was huge, with broad shoulders and massive hands. Taking him on would suck.

"Yeah, that's what, the third one? Thank God, we put them on that small boat when they looked like they were dangerous."

They walked away and towards where I left the other man. Not wasting an opportunity, I slipped inside the open door and pulled the stick away, letting the door close slowly. I eased the door shut as quietly as I could, as I wanted some more time. In the back of my head, I wondered where my dad was and what they were doing. It seemed like there wasn't as much pandemonium as we had hoped for and things were back to normal. I needed to find Ben and finish this.

I moved down a long corridor and decided the time was right for getting serious. I was irritated at not finding Ben, scared about Jake, relieved at finding my father, worried about what Uncle Charlie was going to do to me for having a relationship with his daughter, and frustrated that our big plans were pretty worthless since they were used to things blowing up around here.

I unslung my rifle and remembered the words I once read about the American Revolution. At the opening shots of the war, Captain Parker of the militia told his men, "Don't fire unless fired upon. If they mean to have a war, let it begin here." Ben started this little fracas, and I was done with nice.

CHAPTER 62

I approached a larger hallway, and I could hear voices coming my way. Two men rounded the corner and suddenly stopped, their eyes going wide at the sight of me. Their reflexes were pretty good, as they both reached for the guns on their belts. I fired twice, dropping both men with shots to the chest. The heavy crash of the rifle in the hallway made my ears ring, but the echo of the shots bounced off the walls from the glass of the end hall to the front gate. For a second, all was still, but then all hell broke loose.

Bullets started searching down the hallway, but since I controlled the entrance and no one could flank me, I was in a decent spot. Anyone coming in the front was meat, and if someone tried to come through the back, it was locked. However, that didn't stop some people from shooting down the hallway. I think they were trying for some kind of luck with a ricochet, but that wasn't going to happen with drywall.

I crept forward, and when the occasional shot stopped, I peeked around very quickly. A barrage of firing sent bullets thudding into the wall on the opposite side of the hallway, and I had to chuckle at the attempt.

I pulled one of the guard's guns and stuck it around the corner, shooting it randomly until it ran out of bullets. I heard some cursing and shouting before the shooting started again, so maybe I nicked someone.

Suddenly, there was shouting. "Cease fire! Cease fire!" The shooting stopped and the voice continued. "Who the hell is in that hallway? What do you want?"

I wasn't inclined to make things easy, so I stuck the other guard's gun around the corner and shot it empty, renewing the cursing and sound of scrambling to get out of the way of the flying bullets.

"Stop shooting, you asshole!" The voice yelled. "What the fuck is wrong with you? What do you want?"

I went over to the two dead men, pulled the guns off of them and with a heave, threw one into view of the others. There was a collective gasp and more swearing, and at the pivotal moment, I stuck the dead man's gun around the corner and fired some more. I had to be seriously pissing off everybody.

"Son of a bitch! You'll pay for that!" The man was clearly agitated. "You can't stay in that hallway forever!"

I tossed the second man out and waited. There was no response, which was a concern. I slowly eased away from the wall, keeping an eye on the corner, trying to see them before they saw me.

The cold barrel of a gun on the back of my neck stopped me in my tracks. I raised my hands and was relieved of my rifle. My Beretta was taken from me and my knife and tomahawk were taken as well. My sword was removed, and through all this, my captor didn't say a word. However, the gun on my neck never left for an instant. I kept my hands up, but my mind was a flurry of calculations about how fast I could move and how long it took for a finger to pull a trigger. Every equation I tried had a single answer. I was fucked.

CHAPTER 63

Suddenly, the barrel was lifted and I heard my captor laugh to himself. I turned around and saw three people standing in front of me. Two who were obviously women were pointing rifles at me, and they were the flanking bodyguards of the man who held a small stainless pistol at his side. His white hair looked slightly unkempt, but he was well dressed and well fed.

"Hello, Ben," I said.

"Hello, Aaron," Ben said. "How's your family doing?"

I nearly risked it right then. I calculated the odds and they were really close. If the two guards blinked at the same time, I was going to give it a go.

Trouble was, Ben knew it. He backed up out of reach, and the guards did the same. Ben smirked at me and waved the gun in the direction of a service door that had been cleverly painted to match the wall. I shrugged and walked behind him, still flanked by the guards. They walked behind me and aimed their guns in a cross pattern. They could shoot me and miss Ben, so that opportunity was gone.

Since I wasn't already dead, every moment was an opportunity. I just had to choose the right one. We walked down a dark corridor, past service doors and rear entrances to shops with their names on the doors. At one point, the corridor darkened, and I slowed slightly, but one of the guards jammed the muzzle of her gun into my neck, so that opportunity was wasted. At the end of the corridor, Ben opened a door without looking back and walked through it. I followed and raised my eyes to what must have once been a magnificent sight.

The room was huge, easily the size of a few houses. A gigantic dome rose above two stories of windows, creating a massive space. Outside the windows, I could see the lake, and there were a couple of boats tied to the end of the pier. Ben led me up onto a stage, and directed me to a single chair sitting in the middle of it. I sat down and put my hands in my lap. The guards flanked me again and Ben went over to a small switch on the far wall. He put down my guns, knives, and sword. From my vantage point, I could see nearly one hundred and eighty degrees of the lake. In its day, it must have been beautiful. The sun was getting higher, and the glass was lighting up with multiple hues of blue and green.

Ben walked over to stand in front of me. He still held his gun, and dismissed his guards with a slight turn of his head.

"You've been a pain in the ass, you know that?" He said.

I shrugged. "Likewise. Why did you want to restart the Upheaval?" I asked.

It was Ben's turn to shrug. "Seemed like the thing to do. The original was such a beautiful thing to see, watching society fall apart. I could do anything I wanted and to anyone I wanted. There were no repercussions." Ben's eyes drifted away for a second. "After scratching out a living for years, on the edge of civilized society, suddenly we could take anything we wanted. All we needed to be was more ruthless than the next man was.

"But that all ended when your damned father came marching in with his ideas about restoring the country. Damned fools were so desperate for a leader they took anyone, including that self-righteous bastard Talon." Ben practically spit that last out.

I didn't say anything, as another door on the far side of the stage opened up. Dozens of men and women streamed in, looking about as normal as can be, except they all were wearing a gun and a knife. In addition, they each carried a small pouch on their belts. The pouches looked familiar and I had a feeling I might know what was in them. We never found any syringes at the zombie factory, so it made sense that they were all stored here.

The people kept coming, and when the stream finally slowed, there had to be at least one hundred and fifty people here. One hundred fifty with a gun and knife on each, and likely a way to infect people with refined Enillo Virus. If I thought I was screwed before, I was in for some serious pain now. Everyone sat down in chairs in front of the stage, and they all sat quietly, looking up to their leader.

I didn't see a way out of this one, except for the small ace in the hole I still held. In their relieving me of my weapons, they didn't bother to check my vest, thinking the Beretta was the only gun I had. I still had my dad's .45 in my vest, tucked away out of sight. With my hands on my knees, I could get it out in a second, but would it be enough of a surprise to beat the bullets from the guards that I knew would be coming?

I was afraid I was going to have to find out. A second concern was where the hell was my father?

CHAPTER 64

As the assembled people settled in, Ben spoke. His voice was quiet, but powerful, and easily carried to the corners of the ballroom. "The man sitting here is Aaron. He is the son of my enemy. He has collected from our city without our permission, and he has killed our brothers and sisters. He has thwarted our efforts to return the word to its natural state, and he has destroyed our factory in the south. What shall we do with him?"

A small chorus of 'Kill him' rose from the crowd, but it died away as Ben raised his hands.

"I thought so, but this one's death must be a message. It must be taken with as much care as my brother's was, so many years ago." Ben bowed his head, and the rest of the people did, too.

I had no clue what he was taking about, and wouldn't care if I did. I did know that I saw movement at the back of the hall, and that movement was manifesting itself as two men walking out of the shadows. Both were tall, and walked deliberately, holding powerful rifles at the ready. Other weapons sprouted at various spots on their frames, and even from this distance, I could feel the air change at their approach.

Ben must have, too. He looked up and took a breath to speak, but was cut off.

"Shut the fuck up, Ben," Dad said.

Over one hundred and fifty heads turned, and one hundred and fifty hands reached for guns. However, everyone froze when my Uncle Charlie raised his rifle and shook his head.

My dad continued, "My name is John Talon. This serious-looking gent is Charlie James. We're here for my son, Aaron. Hand him over unharmed, and we'll leave. Cause a fuss, and we'll kill every one of you sons of bitches."

The door by the stage banged open, and Tommy walked through. He was holding what looked to be a belt-fed weapon, and there was a lot of ammo hanging off his shoulder, disappearing into a heavy bag. He walked around the stage and positioned himself to the side of the assembly before he spoke.

"Full-auto, kiddies. Don't even think about it." Tommy spoke with a half smirk on his face, practically daring the assembled people to try something.

Ben stared at the men who had appeared like ghosts in his very hall. I was sure his mind was racing with possible solutions, and I knew he was going to try something.

"You don't have the power you once did, John. You don't get to call the shots this time. Drop your weapons, or by the time I count to three, my guards will shoot your son. One!" Ben shouted the number and all heads swiveled back to my father and his crew. I leaned forward as if I was intently watching my father, but I was trying to mask the movement of my hand into my vest for the other gun.

"Two!" Ben shouted, raising his gun to point it at my dad. I braced my feet and a second later launched myself backwards, drawing the .45 at the same time. My movement carried me behind the guards, and I swung the gun up just as Ben shouted again.

"Three!"

Two shots rang out over the ballroom. Deep, booming shots that ended Ben's countdown. Ben never bothered to turn around. He didn't realize something was wrong until I jammed the warm muzzle of the 1911 into the back of his neck.

"My name is Aaron Talon," I said into his ear. "My father is John Talon. Congratulations. You've managed to piss us both off." I tore Ben's gun out of his hand and backhanded him with the .45, knocking him to the floor. I grabbed a handful of his shirt and heaved him to his feet, shaking him like a rag doll. His head rolled around and his shoulders slumped, but I knew he was still plotting. I wanted to kill him so badly that I could taste it.

I raised the gun but my dad called out.

"Stop, Aaron!" He came walking over, still keeping his gun on the now angry faces of the assembled people. He stepped up to the stage and spoke to the crowd. "I meant what I said. We're leaving. You might want to as well. The front gate has broken, and there's a shitload of hungry zombies headed this way. If you're lucky, you might make it to the large boat and get out of here. Try a shot at us and we'll open fire. Make your choice."

You would have thought someone dropped a skunk in the room. People cleared out faster than I thought they could. There were shouts and screams, but everyone kept moving. In a minute, the ballroom was empty.

My dad walked over to Ben and relieved me of him. He took him to the edge of the stage and threw him off, causing him to land heavily at the feet of Charlie. Charlie searched him quickly, and then dragged him to his feet, tying Ben's hands behind his back. I retrieved my weapons and put them where they belonged. I handed my father his gun back.

He took it with a smile. "When did you learn to shoot like that?" he asked, looking down at the two guards I had killed.

I shook my head. "Luckiest thing I have ever done."

Dad was about to speak when his radio spoke. "John? They're coming. You want to get out of there now. Duncan out."

"Got it. On our way. John out." Dad swung his hand in a circle and everyone started moving towards the back of the ballroom. I could hear a new sound outside, and I knew it for what it was. A horde was coming, and we had nowhere to retreat.

CHAPTER 65

I looked at my father as we reached the back of the room. "What's the plan?" I asked.

Dad shoved Ben outside. "You'll see."

The lake was a beautiful blue this afternoon, with drifting clouds racing each other across the horizon. The back end of the pier was a large walkway and sitting area, where people could just come and sit, once upon a time. Right now, there was a small boat working its way around the corner of the pier, sliding smoothly alongside. Uncle Duncan waved at me with his familiar grin and tossed a line to Uncle Tommy, who threw his heavy weapon and bag over to Duncan.

Dad and Charlie walked Ben out to the pier and Ben had recovered enough of his wits to see what was going on and started screaming. "No! No! You can't! Nooo!" He kicked and heaved, and finally Charlie threw him to the ground and tied his ankles together. He then picked up his feet and dragged the thrashing man the rest of the way.

A single chair had been placed by one of the decorative lampposts that lined the edge of the pier. They were about fifteen feet high and made of copper plated steel. The copper had turned green with age, but this post had an interesting feature. A rope hung from the part of the lamp that stretched over the water, and the other end was waiting by the chair. A noose had been conveniently tied on the near end.

Charlie sat Ben in the chair and flipped the noose around Ben's head. Taking the other end, Charlie pulled Ben to a standing position on the chair and tied off the other end of the rope. When Ben hung, he would swing out over the water, about five feet from the edge of the pier.

Behind us, the moaning was growing louder and louder, and there were shots and screams as Ben's followers encountered the zombies.

My dad positioned himself in front of Ben and looked into Ben's tear-filled eyes.

"You killed families, tried to kill towns. You orphaned dozens of kids and tried to wipe out the communities that survived the Upheaval. You kidnapped young women away from their homes and turned them into virus factories." My father stepped closer and his voice dropped to a harsh whisper. "You tried to kill my sons."

My father turned and walked away, climbing aboard the boat. I stood with Charlie by Ben.

"Zombies are coming, Ben," Charlie said. "You choose. Step off that chair and hang, or stay there and let the zombies eat you." Charlie leaned in. "You tried to kill my daughter. Personally, I hope you don't have the guts to slowly suffocate to death." Charlie walked away and boarded the boat.

Ben looked at me with pleading eyes, but I wasn't having it. "You sent men to infect parents who would then kill their children. I saw it. I was there. Die screaming, you bastard." I walked away and got on the boat myself.

CHAPTER 66

As soon as I boarded, Duncan slipped the lines and we pulled away. We moved about twenty yards away from the pier and waited. Ben twisted a bit, and it looked like he was trying to slip his hands under his feet, but the noose around his neck wouldn't let him. The first zombies appeared around the corner and Ben shrieked at the sight. The ghouls locked onto the meat hanging at the ready and lumbered forward, reaching and grasping. Ben twisted and screamed, and more zombies came around the corner. Just as the first ones were about to reach him, Ben fell off the chair and swung out over the water. His feet kicked and his neck stretched, but he wasn't dead yet. His momentum swung him out and then back towards the pier. The undead reached out and a smaller one of them managed to grab Ben's shirt. The zombie hung on as Ben swung out again, this time with additional weight. The zombie hung on, facing Ben, as he slowly turned purple. The undead leech crawled up Ben, grabbing him by the hair and ear. The zombie reared its head back and took a huge bite out of Ben's face. The kicking kept up as the two swung together for a long time, with the zombie eating the face off the slowly asphyxiating Ben. Blood poured into the waters below. Finally, Ben stopped moving and the zombie continued to feed, tearing of chunks of cheek and face. After a while, the virus reanimated Ben's corpse, and it turned slowly on its leash, swinging with its partner. The extra zombie let go, dropping into the lake and vanishing below the waves.

My father and I watched the whole thing, and when Ben finally turned, Dad shot him in the head. The zombie's head drooped and the body swayed slowly back and forth.

Holstering his gun, my dad signaled to Duncan. "Let's get to the capital. My boy is hurt and I want to see him. This job is done."

I settled in for the long ride home. The last thing I saw of the pier was the corpse of Ben swinging in the breeze.

CHAPTER 67

Jake took three weeks to recover and he was even a bigger pain in the ass. He complained about the pain, and then he complained he couldn't move. Then he complained he moved too much. Dad stayed with him for a solid week until he was certain Jake was going to recover, then the complaining got to him, too. We stayed at the hotel, and to pass the time, my father and I sparred. I didn't see much of my Uncle Charlie, but I spent my nights with a very grateful Julia, who I finally got around to proposing to. She accepted and all was good, but for the one day, Charlie came around.

The day before we were to leave, I was on the back porch of the hotel room getting a little sun in the chill air when someone knocked on the door. Julia was out at the market looking at dresses with Kayla, whom Jake had surprisingly proposed to, and my father was at the president's house as he had been for a few days. So I had no idea who was knocking.

When I opened the door, a huge hand hit my chest and shoved me backwards, sending me across the room. I lost my footing but rolled over, getting to my feet to meet the giant who streaked across the room after me.

Uncle Charlie slammed into me and knocked me into a wall. His left hand was on my throat and his right was holding one of his tomahawks. His hand was high up on the handle, a good grip for precision cutting and punching with the blade. I knew this because Charlie had taught it to me.

"Going to marry my daughter, are you? Think you're good enough?" Charlie asked, glaring into my eyes.

I didn't see any sign that he was kidding around, so I did what I thought was best. I grabbed his right hand and twisted towards the wall, slamming his shoulder into it and loosening his grip on my throat. I leaned to the side to slam an elbow back into his forehead, and then jumped forward to avoid the down stroke of his 'hawk. I spun around and faced my uncle Charlie.

"I don't plan on doing anything but loving your daughter, you damn fool! Knock this off before someone gets hurt," I said, circling around to where my pack and weapons were.

"Yeah, you were loving her all the while I was gone, not waiting to face me," Charlie snarled.

"You were gone!" I shouted. "Dad was gone! We had no one but each other! You want to fight, fine, but by God, you aren't going to get it for free!" I was mad now and pulled my own tomahawk out of my pack. I held it back in my right hand, keeping my left out in front to wait for his attack.

Charlie stepped forward, and pulled his second 'hawk out. "It's about time." He took a step then the axes dropped to his side. He started laughing and I stood there, waiting for some trick. When he looked at me again, he laughed some more, then fell over on his side, laughing harder. I straightened up and frowned as my Dad walked through the door, laughing hard himself.

"What the hell?" I asked to no one in particular.

Dad helped Charlie to his feet, and explained as he wiped away a tear. "Charlie and I couldn't be happier, Aaron. We knew you two would likely get together at some point. It was just natural. Charlie was worried Julia would fall for some townie and want to settle in a community. It's all right."

Charlie rubbed his forehead and thumped my dad on the arm. "The things I have to go through to get a good son-in law.'

"You're lucky. He would have taken you to school," Dad said.

Charlie nodded. "That's for sure."

CHAPTER 68

Julia and I were married in town with her father giving her away. Kayla was the maid of honor, and Jake was my best man. Once we were finished, Jake, Kayla, Julia and I switched places and Jake and Kayla got married. Duncan walked his daughter down the aisle after Uncle Tommy checked his pockets for explosives.

The six of us travelled back to the lodge, and for a week, neither couple left their rooms for much besides eating.

Two weeks after Jake and I were on the back porch, looking out over the tree tops as they lost their last leaves for winter. Distant growls and snarls made us smile as our forest guardians fought over winter food.

"What's the plan, Jake?" I asked suddenly.

"That obvious, is it?" Jake replied.

"Yeah. When are you leaving?" I asked.

"Likely after winter. We'll be heading down the river a ways, then out across the plains. I need to see those mountains, Aaron. I can't explain why." Jake looked west and I could see he was seeing those Rocky Mountains in his mind.

"Well, in order to keep you out of trouble, Julia and I should likely come with you," I said.

Jake turned and faced me. "I can't ask you or her to do that, Aaron."

"You didn't." I grinned. "I told you. Now let's go tell the ladies."

"Dad's going to be pissed," Jake said.

"He and Uncle Charlie have no room to complain. Besides, we'll be back."

"True."

We walked into the main room and called everyone in. When we broke the news Julia and Kayla hugged, and our fathers looked thoughtful. Finally, my dad broke the silence.

"You coming back?" he said.

"Depends," I said.

"On?" Charlie asked.

"How much we might be needed out there," Jake said.

Dad looked at Charlie and they both shrugged.

"Stay in touch," Charlie said.

"Any reason why you're going too, Aaron?" My dad asked.

I smiled. "It's what I do."

THE END

www.ingramcontent.com/pod-product-compliance
Lightning Source LLC
Chambersburg PA
CBHW060431180626
46817CB00007B/2767